Michael Gouda

A Tangled Web

A story of adventure and mixed fortunes

JustFiction Edition

Publisher:
JustFiction! Edition
is a trademark of
International Book Market Service Ltd., member of OmniScriptum Publishing Group
17 Meldrum Street, Beau Bassin 71504, Mauritius

Printed at: see last page
ISBN: 978-613-7-40750-9

A Tangled Web

Michael Gouda

Chapter 1 Kenneth Spiller

Being the runtiest guy ever and not having much brain power, I was never expected to make a great mark on the world. My mother, who preferred gin to me, often told me that I'd never get married as no girl would ever fancy me. My father, before he left the family for ever, told me that, if I didn't either do good at sports or get brainy quick, I might as well give up on the livelihood stakes. As you can see they didn't exactly inspire me with confidence or hope.

But I could see what they meant. My ears stick out like jug handles. Of course Prince Charles' do too but when you're a Prince you can get away with things like that. My hair, which on some guys just seems to naturally fall into attractive positions even (especially) when ruffled, is like lank straw without even the yellow color. Mine is sort of mousy brown. I have a nose and a mouth and two eyes in roughly the appropriate positions but there is a certain lopsidedness about them which gives me a look of impermanence, perhaps incongruity.

I'm using long words because my English teacher at school said I should broaden my vocabulary but sometimes I think I use the wrong words and, now I've left school, there's no one to correct them.

I think I'm quite a kind person if only I could get over this shyness which makes me stutter and stammer whenever I try to speak to strangers. I don't think there's a basic weakness there, as, when I'm on my own, I can speak quite normally – if normal is the word for someone who more often than not talks to himself.

I do have a job which fact would have spited my dad, had he been around to notice, but it was a dead end one, laboring mostly which means making the tea, mixing the 'muck' (our name for plaster), pushing the wheelbarrow etc. – anything that doesn't demand much brainpower. The guys are quite kind but they treat me as if I'm a sort of pet, you know, patting me on the top of the head occasionally – if only I were a foot taller, say 6' 2", they wouldn't do that. They refer to me as 'Chrissy' rather than Chris which makes me feel a bit silly, and sometimes they tease me about not having a girlfriend or being such a wimp when we have a kick around with a football, and not being able to speak up for myself without stammering. It's all kindly meant, I'm sure but deep down it hurts.

Like this morning.

We started a new job. Clearing up a nice middle-class house after it had been devastated by the recent summer floods. Everything downstairs was ruined. There were bookcases and I'd never seen so many books except in the school library, not that I went there much except under protest. This old guy was wandering about in a bit of a daze picking up one book after another, soaked, dripping and mostly covered with a film of, well, not to put too fine a point on it, shit.

"Not a good idea to handle them without gloves, sir," said my boss, Jas. "And make sure you wash your hands thoroughly afterwards. I think most of that came out of the sewers."

The old guy didn't seem to know what was going on. "All gone," he said. "After all these years."

"Make a list of them," said Jas. "You'll be able to claim replacement value."

"Some are irreplaceable," said the guy. There was no answer to that of course.

"Here," said Jas. "Read out the titles and whatever to little Chrissy here. I think he can write."

I suppose it was a joke but neither the old guy nor me found it funny – though probably for different reasons.

In that dirty downstairs room which smelled of damp and mud and worse, while Arthur and Sid carted out damaged armchairs, a desk, a table and modern things like a TV and sound system, I perched on a wooden upright chair whose seat hadn't quite been reached by the flood and with paper and biro wrote down what seemed to be this guy's family and friends. Certainly he was as cut up about losing them as if they'd been real flesh and blood relatives. I could almost understand this.

Sometimes there were tears in his eyes as he announced the name of what must have been real favorites and I nearly said 'They're only books' but restrained myself, not quite sure why because that was only what they were.

"I've been collecting them all my life," he confided. "Probably since I was your age. How old are you?" he suddenly asked almost as if he'd noticed me for the first time.

"Eighteen," I said stoutly. Actually I'm only seventeen but I have problems with 's's so I avoid them when possible.

"Are you?" he said. "I'd have thought you were younger." That because I'm short I suppose.

They weren't a very exciting lot of books. Some of them had the word, 'Antiquities' in the title (I had to ask him how to spell that, and got into a bit of a state over 'spell' but he didn't seem to notice). A lot of them had 'First Edition' added to the title. I wasn't sure what that meant but as there were such a lot of them I decided that, if we wanted to finish the job, we'd better leave conversation out of it. It's not my strong point anyway, as I've already explained.

There were some surprises too, like Rudyard Kipling's 'The Jungle Book' "First Edition, 1894," he said sorrowfully, holding up a tattered copy which dripped mucky water onto the floor. I thought that was a kids' book, and anyway they'd made a film of it so I don't know why he made such a fuss. There'd probably be a paperback version in the local bookshop anyway and he could get that for a couple of quid.

As I said it was a long job and I got a bit fed up with writing, and a touch of writer's cramp, which is like wanker's cramp but not from as satisfying a cause.

Eventually we finished and Jas put me on to mopping up the floor. A shitty job but someone's got to do it. He and the others had a fag and a cuppa outside and then they brought in the dehumidifiers and set them working.

"How long will it be before everything dries out?" asked the old guy.

"A month or so," said Jas, "maybe two. We'll come back and check it out from time to time."

"I could go and stay with my sister," said the old guy. "Except she doesn't like cats."

"Ah," said Jas unhelpfully. I suspected he wasn't really interested in the old guy's problems. He'd got a job to do and he'd done it. Now was time to move to the next one. "Come on, Chrissy, we've got work to do."

As he spoke there was a mewing sound and a cat's head appeared from round the bannister stairs followed by the rest of the animal. It was tabby and surveyed the scene, the still damp floor, the lack of any comfortable furniture, the burly workmen with obvious disapproval.

"Here's Princess," said the old guy. "Come on down. They won't hurt you."

One of the workmen, Alf, barely suppressed a giggle. Calling a cat, Princess! Sad.

The cat though decided that its master's voice meant that all was safe. It came down the remaining steps, trod fastidiously on the floor and then made for me, winding round my legs in an affectionate manner.

"Ah," said the old guy, "a fellow cat lover."

I didn't want to be teased more than ever so I said. "Not really." Then added, so as not to upset the old guy's feelings, "I like all animals." Better than most humans, I could have added. I stroked the cat's head and it pushed it into my hand purring.

"Well, we'll say good-bye for now, Mr Spiller," said Jas. So that was his name.

I gave the cat a last minute stroke and followed the lads out to the van leaving Spiller holding the cat and looking lost and forlorn in the middle of his puddle of a living room.

You might ask why I bothered to relate this little episode if that was all there was to it, but in fact it was only the start of my relationship with Mr Spiller.

A couple of weeks later Jas and I were doing a job, he doing the expert bit (plastering), me mixing the muck (plaster) when, on the way home he suddenly realized he should have called in on Mr Spiller to test the walls. When we got there it didn't look as if much had happened. The room was empty, the kitchen devoid (that's a good word, ain't it?) of all appliances and cupboards. The only bit of comfort was an 'eastern' looking rug, red with a convoluted (wow!) pattern in yellow and blue. On this sat Princess. Clearly she had decided that the dehumidifiers, despite their noise, were good providers of warmth.

Mr Spiller had let us in but it was Princess who greeted me, again winding herself round my legs as cats do and purring loudly. Without the gang I felt able to pet her so I sat down, cross-legged on the rug and Princess came and curled up on my lap, while Jas pushed his damp meter (or whatever it's called) against the walls and muttered readings just under his breath. He wandered into what remained of the kitchen next door.

"Well," said Mr Spiller, "you may not be too fond of cats but she has obviously taken to you."

It's nice when a strange animal thinks you're a friend, so I smiled. "I really prefer dogs, but Princess is nice," and I didn't even stutter over the 's' sounds.

"I have a dog too, but the problem there is taking her out. My leg, you know." He tapped his right leg on the thigh. "It makes walking difficult – and Shannon loves her walks, well, needs them too."

Up until then I hadn't even noticed Mr Spiller limping or anything wrong with his leg but a moment later there was this confusion at the front door which we had left open and a boisterous collie rushed in followed by a young man with bright red cheeks and tousled hair. He was older than I was, probably mid twenties. Like the dog he looked as if he'd been racing over the fields and having a rare old time.

Both pulled up short when they saw there were strangers present. Princess who had looked alarmed at their entry, settled down when she saw who it was, and her calmness seemed to quieten them all down. The dog wagged its tail at me and the guy smiled, a smile which extended to his eyes. He was tall and had short dark hair and his smile revealed white teeth. In comparison I felt runtier than ever.

"Hi," he said, "I'm Dominic."

Well, if that wasn't a poofy name, perhaps not as bad as Chrissy, but well on the way, I don't know what was. "Chris," I said, or attempted to say but the final 's' wouldn't come out. I would have been embarrassed except that at that moment Jas came back in and Shannon obviously took a dislike to him. She barked furiously and growling went towards him.

"Call your dog off," said Jas, clearly alarmed and I grabbed hold of the dog's collar.

"She won't hurt you," I said, the action giving me confidence. "Look she's a complete wimp." Shannon, perhaps realizing that her bluff had been called, wagged her tail, turned round and licked my face.

"You don't know what she's been eating in the field," said Dominic. From the smell, I think I did.

'Sheep shit,' I would have said but I wasn't sure how I'd cope with the consonants at the start of each word.

Peace settled. Mr Spiller thanked Dominic for taking the dog out. "I don't know what I'm going to do the next two weeks when you're on holiday."

"I'm sorry, Kenneth," said Dominic, "but it's been arranged for ever so long. The parents would be disappointed if I didn't go."

"I know," said Spiller. "I'll sort something out. You have a marvelous time. I remember when I went round the Greek islands. Make sure you visit the places I told you about."

"I'd need a year there to do all that," said Dominic, "but I'll do what I can."

He patted the dog, stroked the cat's head, waved at the rest of us and departed with another broad smile.

Shannon whimpered. "She doesn't approve when people she likes leave," said Spiller.

Jas cleared his throat. Clearly he'd decided that he'd not been the centre of attraction for too long. "Not quite dry enough," he said, tapping the walls, "but better than I thought it would be. Perhaps another week and we'll see." He made for the door, then said, "Chrissy!" and went out.

I followed him but then had a thought. I'm not usually one for making sudden, impetuous decisions. I turned. "I could take your dog out," I said. Luckily there were no 's's or I'd have had problems. "Morning and evening, if you like."

"Are you sure?"

I nodded and followed Jas to the van. Shannon whimpered.

"Bloody dogs," said Jas. "They should have them under control."

* * *

Mr Spiller lived in the next village to mine. All the same it was about three miles away but luckily I had an old banger of a bike, one of those almost antique 'sit up and beg' types which I'd found in a skip some years ago. It made awful squeaking sounds when the pedals turned and rattled when it went over uneven surfaces. I was fairly ashamed to be seen on it by any of my contemporaries who used to skim by on mountain bikes or racing models. But there weren't many of those around as I had to set off really early in the morning to get to Spiller's, take Shannon for a decent walk and get back home in time to be picked up by Jas's van at eight o'clock.

Of course it was summer time so it was light by the time I set off at six, made my noisy way down the High Street, onto the side road that led to the next village.

After the first few mornings Shannon would be waiting at the window and as I squeaked into view, she'd bark her welcome and Spiller would be at the open door, smiling and with a mug of coffee and a couple of biscuits ready 'to fortify me for the run' as he put it.

Then, we raced across the fields, scattering the sheep, though Shannon never chased them and they probably enjoyed the run as much as we did. Her favorite walk was down to the stream where we spent a while throwing and retrieving sticks, then back through the wood where we often managed to flush out some pheasants. These Shannon would chase though she never had the slightest chance of catching them, and, when I whistled, she'd come loping back, panting her enjoyment to walk by my side back home.

In the mornings I had to dash back to make sure of being there when Jas arrived of course, but in the evenings, when the daylight was turning to dusk, Spiller would invite me in, ask me to share some food and offer to pay me for the walking. At first I refused the food but, as I got used to Spiller, I accepted, though never the money.

"I like taking Shannon out. It's not a job to be paid for. I'd love a dog of my own."

So in the evenings we would sit there either in the ruined front room (he'd brought in a couple of easy chairs from somewhere) or outside in the lingering sunset on a wooden garden bench with Princess in one of our laps (her choice of course) and Shannon sprawled on the ground by our side. Spiller was drinking coffee, his favorite drink and he'd got me a cola. The flood didn't seem to have done the garden much harm, perhaps the silt had provided some nutrients, and the flowers were out, not that I knew their names, and there was sweet scent from a honeysuckle (which I did recognize) draped over the wall and hanging over our heads.

Spiller would talk of books, which was one of his passions, travel which had been another until his accident which ruined his leg and life in general. I'd listen but not be able to contribute much even though he did ask me questions about myself. It was quiet and peaceful and I enjoyed those evenings. You'd think that Spiller might have come across like a boring old fart but his enthusiasm and the way he described things and places so that you could almost see them made him interesting.

I almost began to understand his passion for old books. "Made with love and real enjoyment for readers who considered them valuable, not like modern ones which are just out for profit, have no craftsmanship at all. Look at this one." He handed me a book which had obviously escaped the flood. Its covers were dark red, almost as if made of leather and the pages inside had a smooth, rich feel to them. The title on the back was in gold and there was a blue ribbon fastened from the spine to mark the place in the book.

"What modern publisher provides you with one of those?" he asked. "They expect you to put a bus ticket or turn down the corner of the page nowadays. Sacrilege!" What's a bus ticket, I wondered but didn't ask.

Shannon suddenly got up and sniffed into the night air. "Lie down, Shannon," said Spiller. Obediently Shannon lay down again but her eyes were fixed on the bushes at the end of the garden. Then there was a disturbance amongst the leaves and a black and white head peered out. I could just make it out through the dusk. I heard Spiller whisper, "Badger."

Then the rest of the animal came out and wandered over the lawn. I could clearly hear it snuffling. I took hold of Shannon's collar and the badger must have seen my movement because it turned and disappeared.

"They don't usually come out when anyone's around, the breeze must be blowing from it to us otherwise it would have smelled us."

I'd only seen badgers before as sad crushed animals on the roadway. I told Spiller this. "Their eyesight isn't all that good and sometimes they wander into the road and that's it."

"Will it come back?"

"Later probably."

I realized that it was already getting late and that I didn't have a light on my bike. "I must go," I said, and didn't stammer.

For a moment Spiller paused as if he was going to suggest some alternative but eventually all he said was, "Be careful."

* * *

One evening in the second week he again asked me about myself looking at me over the rim of his coffee cup. He asked me why I was prepared to come all the way over to take the dog out rather than doing those sorts of things that a guy of my age would normally do.

"Like what?"

"Oh I don't know. Go drinking with your friends, watch television, play computer games, social networking, listen to music."

"I don't get on with people well. They know I'm s... stupid, and telly and computer games are boring."

"You're not stupid, Chris." He never called me Chrissy. "Whatever made you think you were?"

"My dad used to say I was, and I never passed any exams at school."

"What exams did you take?"

"In fact I didn't take any. I skived off on the days I was supposed to."

"That's a great pity."

"Everyone said I wouldn't pass so I didn't bother. I wouldn't mind having taken English but it was on the same day as Maths and I was hopeless at that."

"A great pity," repeated Spiller. "You've got a good vocabulary. I've heard you use it. What about writing?"

"My handwriting's hopeless."

"I meant on a word processor. Do you ever think of writing stories? Or practical things? A journal. What do they call it nowadays, a blog?"

"Haven't got a computer."

"I have. It was upstairs so didn't get damaged in the flood. Do you want to have a go?"

"I wouldn't know what to write about."

"Yes, I often had that problem when I was writing."

I turned to face him and Shannon sat up. The sun was shining on Spiller's face and he didn't look old at all, well you know, middle-aged, sort of thirty or thereabouts. "Yes, I used to write. Not very good novels I'm afraid, but they provided a bit of bread and butter money. Still do in fact though not so much as before."

An author! I was chatting to a real author. Of course that wasn't as exciting as an explorer or something but it was miles better than the sort of celebrity they trot out on the telly and scarcely anyone has heard of. "Have you got any of your own books?"

Spiller grinned ruefully. "Yes. They were upstairs. Only the important books were down and got ruined."

"Can I s... s... see one?" My excitement had brought back my stammer.

"If you really want to."

He led the way upstairs, limping, one step at a time, Shannon and me trailing after. Princess gave us one look and decided to stay where she was. I hadn't been up here before. As far as I could see there were two bedrooms and a bathroom. No fuss or frills. Each room which I glimpsed through the open doors was tidy with windows that overlooked the countryside fields. I wondered whether Spiller sat up here and watched Shannon and me as we raced across the sheep field. Perhaps he wished he too could run with us. One room had more bookcases and one shelf was filled with books the backs of which I could see had, under the titles, the name Kenneth Spiller.

"Gosh," I said. "You've written a lot."

"Probably too many. After a while I found I was repeating myself."

I hesitated, then came out with, "Could I borrow one?"

"You can have one, if you think you'd like it. Let me write in it for you." He chose one of the books, took out his pen and wrote, 'To Chris from Kenneth, with thanks for looking after Shannon.'

"Will that make it more valuable?" I asked, ever the optimist.

He laughed. "Probably the opposite, but you never know."

The computer was in the other smaller room. It was obviously a bedroom as it had a small single bed but in one corner there was a table with the computer on it. "It's not much more than a word processor. No bells and whistles but it did me for writing. Have a go yourself."

I sat myself down. Of course, even though I didn't have a computer of my own, I'd used one at school. You can't get through school these days without using one. I looked at the blank screen. "What shall I write?"

"Whatever you want. Whatever comes into your mind. I'll go and make some coffee."

Even though the kitchen downstairs was a ruin, they had fitted him with a electric ring in the room next door and of course a coffee pot. Spiller was scarcely ever without his coffee.

I thought, then decided that thinking was making it even harder. I typed, 'My name is Chris. I am stupid and I stammer. I like animals and they seem to like me. My mum says I'll never get a girlfriend because I'm ugly.'

Suddenly it all poured out. I wrote about the building guys and how they treated me, not that I minded all that much because they weren't important. I wrote about Spiller and his being a real author and how I took Shannon out morning and evening. I even mentioned Dominic but that reminded me that soon he'd be coming home and presumably my walks with the dog would be unnecessary. That stopped me.

Spiller came back into the room with two steaming mugs of coffee and some biscuits. All of a sudden I realized what I'd been writing and how personal it was. For the moment I forgot how to delete the whole thing. Easiest thing would be just to switch off but on this strange computer I couldn't find the off switch.

Feeling stupid, I tried to hide the screen with my hands.

"It's all right, I won't read it if you don't want me to. Look make yourself a special folder and have your own password so you can keep it private." I chose 'Shannon' for my password which was naive as it was so obvious. But I saved my writing, pathetic as it was, and felt relieved that I hadn't actually deleted it.

"You can carry on if you want another time. That's your own private file."

On the way home with the hoots of the tawny owls echoing from the trees around and a thin sliver of a moon in the sky dead ahead of me, I thought about the writing. Of course it was complete crap but, once started, I'd enjoyed doing it and it had seemed to flow from me almost without my thinking. Was I a writer? Was I as stupid as people seemed to think? Spiller didn't and he was a real writer.

At home I started reading Spiller's book. I thought I might be disappointed, that it would be dull or over literary, you know, too clever by half but it wasn't. It was just like him, enthusiastic and interesting, descriptive in parts but the things he described came alive, and I didn't have to skim over them. It was a sort of crime novel though really the story was about the characters rather than the crime and the solving of it. In fact I was more interested in the characters than the actual story, though I suppose the story was what made me read on well into the night. I was so late that I almost overslept and had to race like a demon to Spiller's in the morning, and poor Shannon had a rather shorter walk than usual.

The following evening after taking Shannon out, I decided to carry on with my own writing. Perhaps if I tried the same thing but structured it a bit better – that was a good word, 'structured', made more of a plan, thought about the words more... I could still write about me, about the things that I knew and people that I'd met... I tapped away, slowly at first with frequent deletions and then with more confidence...

This was my first paragraph:

'Being the runtiest guy ever and not having much brain power, I was never expected to make a great mark on the world. My mother, who preferred gin to me, often told me that I'd never get married as no girl would ever fancy me. My father, before he left the family for ever, told me that, if I didn't either do good at sports or get brainy quick, I might as well give up on the livelihood stakes. As you can see they didn't exactly inspire me with confidence or hope.'

I didn't know whether it was good or bad. I wondered whether to ask Spiller but thought I'd be too embarrassed to watch him looking at my words. In the end I said to him, as I left. "I've written a bit. Could you have a look and tell me what you think. The password's 'Shannon'."

I almost didn't come back the following morning, dreading what he might say but of course that wouldn't have been fair on Shannon but I needn't have worried. Spiller met me with a big smile. "It's good, Chris," he said. "I like some of the phrases and ideas. We can talk about it this evening if you like but I wouldn't change anything."

"But what about the things that aren't written 'proper'?"

"It's you. It expresses your personality, your preoccupations, your worries. You don't want to turn it into someone else's language."

At the door as the dog strained to be away, he said. "Incidentally your ears. If you're really worried about them, grow your hair longer. It'll hide them even though I personally can't see much wrong with them anyway."

I changed the subject; I don't like talking about my ears. But in fact it sounded like good advice. I was due for a haircut anyway and was going to have the usual short back and sides. Perhaps I'd let it grow but then it would just flop around, long lanks of straw and I'd look a complete dickhead, as if I didn't anyway. There are ways of making hair look thicker and less straight but I'd always been led to think of them as poofy, and anyway my usual barber wasn't the sort to know about things like that. I'd have to go to the 'unisex salon' in the neighboring town and I wasn't sure about that.

In the evening we talked about 'literary matters'. That sounds good doesn't it? Spiller told me about the things he liked about my writing and I decided to carry it on further. I talked about how much I was enjoying his book and the characters. "They seem so real.

"Oh they are. I based them on people I know."

"Even the bad people? Didn't they sue?"

"Are there any bad people? Surely everyone's a mixture."

"The two guys who are living together. You make them sound like a married couple."

"Is that bad?"

I was confused, almost embarrassed. All of a sudden I realized that they were a couple of queers and everyone said that was bad. I bent down and fondled Shannon's ears. I didn't want to answer but Spiller insisted.

"They are supposed to be in love with each other. Is that bad?"

I'd never really thought about it. I couldn't imagine being in love with anyone, much less another guy and mother had said, and I believed her, that no girl would ever fall for me. Of course I'd had sexual feelings. I was seventeen after all and I'd wanked myself silly when I was fifteen and sixteen, but it was only me and my hand and the relief when I came. I may have been naive but I'd never thought of doing it with someone else, never imagined someone else's hand round my cock or putting it anywhere in particular.

"Everyone says it is," I mumbled.

Spiller looked at me. "Everyone?"

"Well, you know ..." Who did I mean? A couple of guys from school who were always together who mocked queers but were always goosing people just for fun. A teacher who had said the most sinful thing for which there was no forgiveness was lying with a man and this was an 'abomination'.

"The Bible says it's an abomination."

"Ah, Leviticus. If you read on it also says 'You shall not cut the hair on the sides of your heads, neither shall you clip off the edge of your beard'. And you've been doing the first of these for a long time."

He smiled and I smiled, Princess yowled for some food and Shannon looked hopeful.

And so the fortnight passed.

On the last Friday Spiller said, "Dominic will be back tomorrow. I expect he'll be taking Shannon out for me." He could obviously see my disappointment because he added, "Perhaps you can both take the dog out."

I thought of Dominic. I'd only seen him just the once but I remembered him vividly. Tall and dark haired, a big smile that seemed to take in everyone. When I'd seen him, out of breath from running with Shannon. I'd felt so insecure beside him. I couldn't imagine that he would want me tagging along.

"I'll see," I said.

Chapter 2 Dominic

In fact I stayed away that first day of Dominic's return but I wanted to carry on with my writing. I'd got to the time where I first met Kenneth Spiller. My memories were clear and I wanted to get them down. The following day was Sunday so there was no work and I left it until well into the morning before I cycled over assuming that Dominic would have taken Shannon out and then gone to wherever Dominic went and did during the rest of the day.

"I may be out all day," I said to Mam and she just nodded.

"Don't know why you bother to come back at all."

Perhaps one day I won't, I thought, though I didn't say it.

Spiller and Princess were in but no Shannon. "Dominic always takes Shannon for an extra long walk on Sundays."

I hadn't known this or I would have done so too.

"She missed you yesterday."

I wondered how he knew that. Today he looked younger, happier and I thought it might have been because Dominic had come back. Did I feel a twinge of jealousy? Of course not. Dominic was Spiller's friend. He called him Kenneth which I had never dared to, nor been asked to, though he had inscribed the book 'from Kenneth'. I'd finished the book by now. The two men friends with whom I'd had that bit of trouble were obviously gay but weren't major characters in the story. I guess they were there just to provide red herrings; they might have been the villains of the plot but in actual fact weren't. Spiller had treated them very sympathetically and, in a strange way, I was pleased that they ended up happily living together in some sort of connubial bliss. I wished that other people had as good relations whatever the gender of their partners.

In the downstairs room they, another group of Jas's men, had started decorating. The walls were painted and the skirting boards in. All looked fresh and clean and only the two old chairs that Spiller had brought in looked out of place. He was sitting in one of them and glancing out of the window from time to time.

"Is it all right if I carry on writing?" I asked.

"Of course. Go on up."

I booted up the computer and found my piece of writing. I typed:

'Spiller was a man of about thirty possibly forty. It was difficult to tell. When I had first met him, distracted and obviously shocked by the results of the flooding, he'd looked really old, his face grey and lined. Later on, after we'd become sort of friends and used to sit in the evening sunshine, he looked much younger, in spite of his hair, grey at the temples and the lines around his mouth which just seemed to emphasize his occasional smile.'

What now? What more was there to say? Nothing had really happened. There was no plot, no story line. Real life wasn't as exciting as fiction, not for me at any rate.

Then, there was a commotion from downstairs. I could hear Shannon's nails scrabbling over the still bare floor boards and a cheerful shout. Dominic was back. I wondered, if I stayed up here, I could avoid meeting him, but it was not to be.

Clearly Shannon recognized that someone was here, probably smelled me and I heard her bounding up the stairs and next she flung herself at me, tail wagging, tongue licking me – she was a very 'licky' dog. Then, after the greeting, she went to the top of the stairs and turned back to look at me. Clearly she wanted everyone to be together.

Okay, I was found out. I switched off the computer and went downstairs.

Spiller was still sitting down and Dominic was standing at the doorway. He looked as I remembered him, tall and dark-haired but now his face was tanned by the presumably Aegean sun. He was wearing a white T-shirt and shorts and his arms and legs were bronzed. I wondered how far the tan went and then wondered why I had wondered such an odd thing.

"You remember Chris," said Spiller, more of a statement than a question.

"Of course. I hear you've been doing my job taking Shannon out. I'm glad. I felt guilty about leaving her."

I stood at the bottom of the stairs feeling stupid and awkward, not knowing what to say.

"She's an affectionate dog, isn't she?" he said and I nodded, not trusting myself to say anything.

"Kenneth suggested you might like to make up a third sometimes."

I shrugged ungraciously, not knowing if he'd been 'persuaded' to make the offer.

"Perhaps," said Spiller, "in the evenings so you don't have to make such a rush job in the morning before work." Though he was talking to me, I noticed his eyes never left Dominic's face.

"Great idea. What do you say, Chris?' Dominic looked me full in the face and I noticed how blue his eyes were, an unusually deep blue. I couldn't hold them and I looked away "Okay." I said or probably mumbled.

So that was my second meeting with Dominic. He left soon afterwards and Spiller watched him intently as he went out through the garden, turned left on the road and disappeared. Shannon whimpered as she always did when someone she liked left, and I had an odd thought that Spiller felt the same way.

Once he was gone, though, I cheered up. "Tell me about him."

"Dominic? Kind, cheerful, reliable, friendly, honest. What more can you want?"

And tall and sexy and good-looking, I thought. And no sticking out ears.

"He lives just down the road with his parents. They own a second-hand bookshop in Chessingham and he works there. That's where I met them though of course I'd noticed him around the village before."

"Do you think he really wants me tagging along with him on a walk?"

"He wouldn't say so if he didn't."

"I thought you might have put him up to it."

"Well, I told him you'd been taking Shannon out while he was away, and that you were disappointed when it might be stopped, but it was his suggestion."

I stayed the day at Spiller's and worked on my story, including some of the early part that I'd left out before, school and such. I almost launched into fiction by writing about a walk with Dominic but found myself suddenly flustered as I wasn't sure what might happen. What could happen except that we walked the dog, I got tongue-tied and it was all a dreadful mistake?

Spiller cooked some food, or rather heated up some ready prepared meals in the microwave which was also upstairs. We had fruit and yoghurt for afters.

"Thank God they're making a real start downstairs tomorrow."

"Yes, I know, I'm part of the team."

After the meal we sat in the sun outside until I started getting a bit restless, wanting to do something. "Care to do a bit of gardening?" asked Spiller. "It's getting really overgrown."

"I don't think I know much about plants. I'd probably pull up the good stuff and look after the weeds. But I'll have a go if you tell me what to do."

Under his direction, I cut back some of the shrubs. He told me their names. There was a viburnum and a choisya and a hebe but I forget the rest. Shannon rooted in the undergrowth looking for anything that made a rustling sound.

"Time for tea," Spiller said eventually. "Or would you prefer a cold drink."

Dead on time Dominic arrived bearing some cans of drink, straight from the fridge, the outsides still frosted. Shannon jumped up joyfully.

"You look as if you've been working hard," he said to me. I felt pleasure at his notice and smiled, for the first time a genuine smile for him.

Afterwards he said, "Come on. Let's not waste this beautiful day. Shannon would like a swim in the stream. Oh, and Kenneth, Dad says he's got some books you'd probably be interested in if you care to drop in this evening."

"Start my collection again? I'll see. But I'd like to chat to your parents about Greece."

"Beware, they'll probably want to show you the photos. Me on Naxos, Dad and mum on Ios. You know the sort of thing."

Shannon, who had heard her name, was already bouncing with excitement. Feeling strangely excited myself, I walked with them into the fields.

It was indeed a beautiful day. A few cotton wool clouds broke up the intense blue of the sky. The grass in the fields was still fresh green after some overnight showers, the right time for rain to fall, as Spiller had said. Along the edges of the footpath were some blue flowers. "Meadow cranesbill," said Dominic. Why did everyone know more than me? But he didn't parade his knowledge. just treated it casually and most of the time he chattered on about his holiday, the places he'd seen and the people he'd met, guys dancing in a ring at a drinking place, the cats, lean and scrawny which were everywhere the only sad thing he'd seen, such a contrast to the pampered Princess.

Soon I didn't feel shy at all, even prompted him with some questions and told him how much I'd like to go abroad, visit strange and wonderful places.

"They don't get much better than this," he said as we reached the stream and sat down on the bank. We threw a stick for Shannon who seemed tireless in her chasing of it, bringing it back to us and laying it at our feet again and again. Eventually even she decided enough was enough and lay down in the shade of an alder tree and panted. Dominic took off his T-shirt and lay back in the sunshine. His chest was tanned and the golden brown disappeared under the waistband of his shorts. The same with the tan on his legs. There didn't seem to be any pale marks at all. Had he been sunbathing naked? I nearly asked him but suddenly got shy.

"What about you?" he asked.

I didn't really know what he meant. I'd told 'about me' on the computer. I couldn't tell him. "Oh, I'm nothing."

"What do you mean? You're you, you have a personality, an individuality, a past, a present and a future."

Well, not much of the last if my father's prophecy was true.

"I'm nothing to look at."

He rolled over and hoisted himself on his elbow, looking at me closely. "Rubbish," he said. "You're cute."

'Cute!' No one had ever said that before. What could he see that no one else had done before? "My ears stick out."

To my surprise, he reached over and with his free hand he touched one of my ears gently, rubbing it between finger and thumb. "Only a bit, and they're beautifully formed. If you want to, you can hide them with your hair. It's long enough."

I had to look away. "It's too long and straight." What on Earth were we doing? Discussing hairstyles like a couple of girls.

"It needs something to thicken it out. A stylist could do it easy."

"I can see that going down a bomb with my Elmcombe barber."

Dominic laughed. "Come to Chessingham next time I go and we'll go to the unisex shop. We'll have you looking like a killer before you know it."

Suddenly his hand slipped down to hold my chin so that I couldn't look away. "Lots of potential," he said quietly, almost as if he was talking to himself. Then he touched my cheek with the palm of his hand and for a moment I didn't know what he was going to do. But he just jumped to his feet and whistled for Shannon. In one way I was relieved, but in another I was disappointed. Though what I had wanted him to do, I didn't know.

It was almost dark when we got back to Spiller's. Dominic came in for coffee and I didn't want to leave him so I came too. Spiller bustled round filling cups and putting biscuits on a plate.

"Well," said Dominic. "Did you get the full photographic treatment?"

"Oh yes. But I enjoyed it. Some of the places were so familiar. And I even pinched a photo of you." He held up the picture. On it Dominic stood in front of a column of some sort. He was smiling and looked so handsome. "I'll have it framed."

"No need," said Dominic, "when you've got the real thing."

There was some spark between them which I recognized but couldn't identify. The two of them sat and talked and occasionally included me. I didn't exactly feel left out because I knew they were friends and had been for some time. Perhaps one day I'd be included in that special friendship.

Eventually Dominic said he had to go and looking out of the window I realized that it was pitch dark. "I'll have to go too."

"You can't cycle with no lights through this," said Spiller.

"I can walk then."

"Why not stay here? There's the bed in the computer room. Only thing is won't your mother worry."

I laughed. "I doubt whether she'd even notice."

"That's sad. Well, if you're sure, you're perfectly welcome."

He limped off with Dominic and I heard them chatting together outside. Then there was silence but it was a little while before Spiller came in. He found me a sleeping bag which was okay with me and I slept well until I awoke at my usual time of six o'clock and had to cycle home to wait for Jas and the gang.

* * *

There was a new guy at work, about my age, called Rick who, if anything was even shyer than me. The guys called him 'Prick' and teased him. In a way I was glad they'd stopped with me but I was sorry for Rick. "It's all in fun, you know," I said to him when we were alone for a moment and he looked grateful.

The following Saturday was a free day. We didn't work Saturdays unless there was a special rush job and obviously there wasn't this week. I decided to go into Chessingham on my own. I'd feel even more of a fool if I had to rely on Dominic shepherding me around like an anxious parent. I could quite easily explain in the hair salon what I wanted. Unfortunately it wasn't as easy as I thought.

My stammer came back when I tried to say. "Can you do s... s... something about my hair to hide my ears. They s... s... stick out." Eventually though I got it out and the girl – yes it was a female – understood what I wanted.

"No problem."

I thought I'd be terribly embarrassed but I saw there were other blokes also having their hair done, even put in curlers, so it wasn't so bad.

"What about a bit of color?" she asked. "Brighten up the hair?"

"Okay." What had I let myself in for? "Not too bright though."

"Trust me, I'm a hair stylist."

Well, I was quite amazed. After she had finished, an hour or so later, the barber in Elmcombe takes ten minutes max, and everything brushed out or whatever, my ears had practically disappeared. And there were gold highlights amongst the 'mouse' which wasn't even mousy even more.

Of course I was even more amazed at the cost but I'd just been paid so I pretended that thirty quid was what I usually paid for having my hair done.

It made a complete difference and I kept catching myself looking at my reflection in the shop windows as I walked back to catch the bus home.

Even Mam noticed and I think she approved. "Almost presentable," she said and then said she was off out to the pub, which was quite okay by me.

I got out my bike and pedaled off to Spiller's. My hair felt different as the wind rushed through it. I hoped it wouldn't take the curl or waves or whatever out of it. Didn't of course. In fact when I got there and saw myself in the mirror I realized that somehow that magician of a girl had given me the sort of hair that looked good even (especially) when ruffled.

During the week there'd been improvements made on the house. The painting downstairs was done, the kitchen had been rebuilt and Spiller was struggling with some new furniture that had been delivered. His leg was causing problems and he looked so harassed that he didn't even notice the improvements in me.

Dominic did, though. "Wow, who's a hottie? So you snuck off without waiting for me. Good for you. You look really good. Doesn't he, Kenneth?"

Spiller then had to take notice. "Why, yes, but I liked your ears as they were."

"He hasn't actually had anything done to his ears," said Dominic.

We sorted out his furniture and downstairs began to look almost presentable though the replacement bookcases looked desperately bare without the books. "You'll soon fill them up. Mum and Dad'll see to that."

Shannon was obviously fed up with furniture removals and was anxious to be out, so we left Spiller in his refurbished rooms and went out.

Dominic and I walked side by side, occasionally our arms brushing companionably. We aimed for the top of Staymore Hill. Half way up Dominic said, "Race you to the top. I'll give you a hundred yards start."

"I don't need your charity," I said and set off, leaving him behind.

"I heard a shout from behind but Shannon was way ahead and I was already puffed and still nowhere near the top. Dominic overtook me and collapsed breathing heavily. Here the wind gusted, blowing aside for a moment the burden of everyday pressure and responsibility. It was like being on top of the world.

"You cheated," said Dominic, still panting, "but I won anyway."

I thought for an answer but could only come up with "I'm cuter than you now."

"Cheeky sod. You deserve getting taken down a peg or two."

He launched himself at my legs and pulled them so that I fell on to my back in the grass. I thought at first that he was angry but I could hear his laughter so I grabbed at him, pulling him down across me. We grappled. He was strong but I was equal to him, weeks of shifting heavy weights had toughened my muscles.

He smelled of soap and healthy sweat and his body was lying across me. My arms were round his chest and I hoisted my legs so that they trapped his body. I was laughing and then so was he. Was he having fun as his body wound itself round and across mine, arms and legs grasping, parts of us pressed together for a while until we struggled free to try another position.

I was certainly having fun. I was getting excited. Wrong! I was excited. I had a real hardon though I tried to avoid letting Dominic know. I could smell him, the clean, fresh smell of him and feel his body against mine.

He smelled of clean soap and something special which was Dominic, slightly musky, sweet. Once when we were especially close I could swear there was an answering hardness but it may have been his hip. His leg was over me and he must surely have been able to feel my own erection.

Suddenly he clasped me even harder, pulled me, if possible, closer. He was no longer smiling or laughing. Then he released me and almost pushed me away

"We must get back," he said, almost a cry.

And so we trailed back in silence, Shannon looking anxiously up at one or the other as if she knew something was wrong. Was there? I didn't know. I was confused, confused about what I had felt when I was wrestling with Dominic, confused about what he had felt. And yet I couldn't say anything and he didn't either.

Again it was dark when we got back. We'd gone further than we had meant to and again I stayed in Spiller's spare room. I didn't sleep well but towards dawn I dropped off and had weird dreams about Dominic and Spiller and me all together, rolling round and round so that I didn't know what was what, who was who.

I was suddenly awakened by the sound of the front door either shutting or opening. Feeling somewhat confused I went to the window and saw Dominic, Dominic leaving and Spiller standing just outside watching him go. At the turn of the gate Dominic turned and waved, then he must have seen me at the window because he suddenly raced off down the road and out of sight.

For a moment I didn't understand and then suddenly realized. Like me, Dominic had stayed the night but he had stayed in Spiller's room. In Spiller's bed? Must be for there was only one double there.

I dressed quickly and went downstairs. Only Shannon and Princess were up and only Shannon whimpered his good-bye as I got onto my bike and cycled noisily off into the dawn. Spiller must have heard me leaving but he didn't appear.

* * *

That week the new lad, Rick, and I were assigned to another group and we didn't work on Spiller's cottage at all. In fact we were sent to a property in the next county and got back so late each day that it was impossible to get over to take Shannon out. I phoned Spiller to explain and he said, "Come as soon as you can. Shannon will miss you." Not Spiller, himself, nor Dominic.

When I did eventually go over there, I found everything changed – and I mean everything. The cottage was repaired. It smelled of paint and newness and downstairs was furnished, even some books in the new bookcases.

Shannon welcomed me as if I'd been gone for years. Perhaps in her world I had and Princess wound herself round my legs. "Where's Dominic?" I asked.

"Things have changed since you were last here. Dominic, his parents and I have gone into partnership. We're moving to Hay on Wye." He sounded excited but I didn't understand.

"Hay on Why?" The words didn't mean anything to me.

"Yes. Don't you know it? A little town on the borders of England and Wales, on the river Wye of course. It's known as the 'book town of England'. It has a Literary Festival every year which Bill Clinton described as 'the Woodstock of the Mind'."

I still didn't understand. "What are you going there for?"

"We're buying a shop. Dominic's parents are selling theirs in Chessingham, and their house here and I'll sell this cottage. It's what I've always wanted to do, deal in books, second hand books."

"And Dominic?"

"Dominic will come with me, with us of course."

"When are you going?"

"A few weeks. It will take a little time to settle up and everything."

It was all too much for me. "I'll take s... s... Shannon out, s... s... shall I?"

The dog, hearing her name, bounded about. Crossing the fields she raced ahead and then came back, tail wagging. To be like a dog who only cares for the present, doesn't worry about the future as long as there's food and company, doesn't care about the past – that must be a good life.

I didn't know about Dominic and me, perhaps there was no Dominic and me, or Dominic and Spiller. There was certainly a Dominic and Spiller though I didn't really know what it was. All I knew was that I was going to be excluded from it. And I didn't really know about me and me, though I did know that I didn't look as ghastly as I'd thought I did, or that I wasn't quite as stupid.

"You'll be all right," I said to the dog. "I expect Hay on Wye has lots of countryside around, and there's a river to swim in, and you'll have Dominic to take you for walks and Spiller to feed you."

"What I want to know is what about me? Do I really like other men or was what happened with Dominic just a reaction to another body? If I'm gay, does it really matter? At least they've shown me I'm not as useless as I thought. I can get on with my life."

Shannon gave me a quizzical look as if to say, 'What's the matter with you? Here's the stream. Find me a stick to throw and I'll jump in and bring it back for you. Life is so simple.'

So I did.

Chapter 3 Rick

I look at myself in the mirror. Dominic had once called me 'cute' but I can't see it myself. My ears are still too big and though now I've grown my hair and had it styled so that most of the jug handle-like projections are hidden, I don't see how anyone can really think I'm attractive.

"When you've finished admiring yourself," says Mum sharply from the kitchen, "perhaps you'll give me a hand taking out the rubbish."

'Giving a hand' of course means doing the whole job but it's easier to do it than start to argue and have a row. After all my mother will soon be off to the pub in Chessingham and I'll be free to do as I want for the remainder of the evening.

What I plan to do is go over to see my friend, Rick. My friend? Is Rick a 'friend'? How long do you have to know someone before you can call him a friend? Like me he's the new workman (builders' assistant) and the others tease him, as they had teased me once, because Rick is quiet and doesn't push himself forward, doesn't boast about his girls, or how much he'd drunk the previous weekend. Do I even like him or is it that I feel sorry for him?

Anyway us two losers sort of stick together and he's asked me over to his house to go with him to take their dog for a walk – a pretty lame occupation for a Saturday night, but there it is and I haven't had a better offer, or even an offer at all.

Rick has a springer spaniel pup, liver and white, according to him. I like animals so I was fairly enthusiastic. I wouldn't mind having a dog myself except I knew Mum wouldn't allow it. 'Too much trouble,' she'd say, 'and all the mess. And you being out all day. I'd have to look after it which I suppose was probably true.

I still wasn't sure about the relationship between Kenneth (yes, I'd got round to calling him by his first name now) and Dominic. But it was not the sort of thing you can ask your mother though, especially mine, or your boss, or your work mates, and I knew no one else. Like the dreadful travesty of a queer in 'Little Britain', if I was, was I the only gay in the village?

And Rick! Yes, what about Rick? He's a nice enough guy when you get below the shy surface. Physically quite stocky, a face, much younger looking than his developed figure suggested. Fresh-complexioned with freckles around his nose. His mouth shows white teeth. When he smiles immediately his rather ordinary looking face is attractive in a masculine way. His eyes are green. The turned-up ends of his mouth make comma-shaped dimples just under his cheek bones.

I want to be a writer so I notice these things. Kenneth, before he left the neighborhood, gave me his computer. It isn't a very modern one but it's okay for word-processing, and I write my thoughts down from time to time. I'm trying to turn them into a story, perhaps even a novel but at the moment, it's all just vague and unstructured.

But do I fancy Rick? That's a real question. Certainly I like being with him. We pal up together when we're at work. So far I've never been really alone with him so today's going to be a first. To be honest I'm getting quite nervous and when I'm nervous, I start to stammer.

It's going to be a disaster I know. Perhaps it would be better to give him a ring and say I can't make it. Yet, he's only a bloke, a bloke I think I like so what's the point in giving up like this?

Having made the decision I worry about what to wear.

I have a shower first and then feel that a blue shirt and dark trousers are suitable – for taking a dog for a walk? Completely wrong. I'm not obsessed with clothes or designer labels and stuff but I like to look as good as possible. I change to some jeans. They cling tightly to my thighs and the outline of my cock and balls show. Are they too obvious? Will they scandalize Rick rather than turning him on? Is he even gay? Am I? Jesus, life is just too fucking complicated. I arrange myself so that I'm not too conspicuous. My chest isn't too bad, all the lifting I do, and the T-shirt shows off what muscles I have. Is white a good color? Perhaps a blue one which matches my eyes will be better.

If I don't hurry, he'll have given up and gone off without me. So, ready or not, I'm off.

A pleasant evening! Midsummer and the air is warm and has traces of flower scents in it. Further down the road, someone has just mown their lawn and the cut grass smells sharp, acrid and a bit metallic. I rehearse what I will say to Rick but hope that the dog will provide the best subject for conversation, otherwise it'll just be about work and that'll be really boring.

It's just after eight o'clock when I get to his house, a modest semi-detached council house, like mine. Still two hours of daylight to go. My ring on the doorbell seems to echo through the house, almost as if it's empty. I wonder if I'm too late and he's taken the dog out already, but then I hear footsteps and hear his voice. "Get out of the way, Sal."

The door opens and Rick is there, a broad smile of welcome on his face. The dog rushes at me, jumping up, her mouth also open as if she's smiling too.

"Down, Sal," says Rick. "She's not very well trained, I'm afraid, just pleased to see visitors."

I bend down and make a fuss of her, rubbing her ears. "She's a grand dog," I notice that I'm not stammering at all.

Rick is wearing a loose T-shirt and baggy jeans which show nothing. They look expensive. He glances at my crotch but I can't interpret his reaction. He shouts back into the house. "We're off, Mum. Don't know how long we'll be."

A woman's voice answers from somewhere in the back but I can't make out exactly what she says. Rick obviously does, because he says. "Okay. Will do."

We set off over the stile and into the fields at the back of the house. That's the beauty of living in a small village, you're so close to the countryside. That's probably the only advantage. There's no clubs, or movies, just a pub, a church, a mobile library which comes round twice a week and a couple of shops which close at five o'clock.

Sal is off, rooting into the undergrowth, looking for something to chase. She really is uncontrollable. Rick and I are a bit shy together – it's the first time we've really been alone – but soon we are chatting, about the dog, and the countryside and eventually about ourselves. Unlike me he's got a mother who cares about him, and a father who's at home and with whom he's on good terms. He also has a younger sister who, according to Rick is a real pain, but that's just sibling rivalry I say to myself knowledgeably.

Away from the gang at work and once the ice is broken, Rick is a fun guy. He makes jokes and I tease him about having a mad dog and, best of all, he doesn't mention my ears.

Soon we're striding over the moor and larks are rising, singing their little hearts out as they climb into the air and hang suspended so far up. I wonder how they can do it, all that wing flapping and singing away at the same time. Don't they ever get out of breath?

Sal finds a stream and plunges in then comes out and shakes herself over the two of us. We tell her off but don't really mean it. The air is still warm and the drops of water soon dry. But the sun is getting low over the horizon and we turn back, in my case reluctantly. And I think that Rick has enjoyed the walk. In fact I know he has because he says, "We must do this again."

Back at his house, Rick says, "Mum told me to ask you in. Come and meet her. She's a bit mad but fairly harmless."

Is this like meeting the in-laws? Okay that was a joke but I do feel that Rick and I are getting close. I put my arm round his shoulders as we go up the path and he doesn't shake it off, just turns his face to me and smiles.

I guess the house isn't much different from mine but the atmosphere is. Though there's some things scattered about, for instance a coat thrown over the back of a chair, some books and magazines lying haphazardly on a coffee table, it's not the same sort of clutter I'm used to. And there's a good smell of cooking in the air and not just fried chips and pizza.

Rick's mother comes out of what is presumably the kitchen. She has a lot of red, frizzled hair and Rick's smile. I realize that I don't know Rick's surname so can't say anything except, "Hello." Perhaps that's a good thing as surely I'd have problems with saying 'Mrs'.

"Can you stay for a meal, Chris?" she asks. "We've got plenty."

I nod and say, "Thank you."

"Had you better tell someone?"

"No one's expecting me," I say, getting it out without much trouble.

She gives me a sharp look but doesn't say anything.

So we sit around the table in the kitchen with an Aga giving out some unnecessary heat. There's Rick and me and the sister whose name is Katie, and his father and mother. Mr – I really must find out Rick's surname – looks prosperous and well-scrubbed. He's changed out of his suit which was what he was wearing when I first saw him and now wears slacks and a polo-necked sweater. He's so obviously professional class that I'm really surprised that Rick is working on the same dead end job as I am. I must ask him about this first chance I get.

We have soup, and a tuna and chicken bake and finally some posh yoghurt, caramel flavored. I could get used to eating like this but probably won't have the chance. My Mum's into chips and convenience foods.

Conversation flows freely over the meal with Katie being particularly curious about me until her mother tells her not to subject me to such an Inquisition. Rick chatters away about work and how I'm the only real friend he has. I get a bit embarrassed but it's nice to hear. I look at him and think he's really good-looking. I like the way his biceps bulge under his T-shirt. I suddenly decide I fancy him. Almost as if he knows what I'm thinking he looks at me and winks.

Katie, of course, notices. "What you winking at him for?"

I'm embarrassed but he isn't. "Because he's my friend."

Afterwards he says, "Do you have to go home yet?" We're both seventeen and shouldn't have to ask questions like that. We could be out roaring round the town, going into neighboring Chessingham and visiting the clubs, getting drunk and throwing up in the gutter. Perhaps even getting into fights. Well, perhaps not the last.

"No."

"Let's go and have a drink."

At the moment the minimum drinking age is eighteen, though they're talking about putting it up to twenty-one. Admittedly many guys can get served under that age but I'm a short person. I probably look younger than eighteen. It's embarrassing to get refused in a pub. Anyway I haven't got all that much money. Both Rick and I are on minimum wage and that for sixteen/seventeen year olds is only £6.70 per hour. After my eighteenth birthday that goes up to £7.60 per hour. Big Deal! So I'm not exactly flush with money.

I explain this to Rick but he says, "No worries. I've got plenty. They'll serve us at the Fish and Griddle, no trouble."

The Fish and Griddle is our local pub. I've been in a few times but not all that often. It's a bit spit and sawdust but it smells better now than it did before the no smoking regulations came into force. Sometimes it has a pianist who pounds out old songs and people sing. Mostly out of tune of course, but it seems to be popular especially towards the end of the evening. The guy who plays is old and doesn't have too much talent. His left hand vamps away, only occasionally making an accompaniment to the tune. The clients buy him pints so that at the end of the evening his playing is even more erratic.

To my surprise Rick seems to be known, at least by the barman. whom he addresses as Dan and gets served without any trouble buying a pint of lager for me as well. We take them over to a table in the corner and sit opposite each other, our knees touching.

"Do you come here often?" I ask and then realize how trite that sounds, like a stale pickup line.

Rick, though, doesn't seem to notice. "Quite often." I don't really understand. Rick seems so completely different from the guy who gets teased at work, the quiet guy with nothing to say. Here he is self-confident, very much in charge, with money to spend and no hang-ups at all.

"What's the attraction?"

He gives me a strange sort of look which I don't really understand and then says, "Well, Dan's quite a nice guy."

It takes me a moment to think who Dan is and then I remember he's the barman. I look over at him. He's probably in his mid-twenties and has very blond hair. He's nice looking and for a moment I'm reminded of Dominic. It isn't so much his looks as the fluid way he moves.

"Are you two friends?"

"Oh, Dan's a very friendly person."

Suddenly I realize I'm being incredibly naive. There is, must be, has been something between Dan and Rick. That's surely what he's telling me. Rick must be gay and, as if to confirm this, I feel Rick's legs under the table imprison one of mine. His hand touches my knee and moves up my thigh.

I gasp. I don't know what is happening but whatever it is, it's here in this public place and I suddenly feel that the table top is transparent, that everyone can see. All the same it doesn't stop me from getting a terrific hard on. I want him to touch me, hold me but I see Dan, from behind the bar looking over at us and I'm sure he knows what's going on and doesn't altogether like it.

"S... s... stop," I start to say. But from his side of the table, Rick can just reach with his fingertips my prick and he knows I'm hard. Gently he touches me, strokes me and I sink down in the seat so that I'm nearer to him, so that he can actually grab hold.

"Are you sure you want me to stop?" He is smiling and I am lost. I put my hand over his and press him into me. He moves his hand up and down and I close my eyes, feeling an orgasm build up inside me. I know the effects will show in my jeans but I don't care.

A voice. "You guys enjoying yourselves?" I open my eyes. Dan is standing beside the table looking down at us. Rick's hand withdraws and I feel my erection wither. Just in time, or just at the wrong time - whichever way you look at it, except that, thank heavens, no one is looking at it.

Dan doesn't wait for an answer but says to Rick, "Budge up." He sits down beside him, close, and I can imagine his thigh pressing up against Rick's.

His hands are below the level of the table top and I wonder if one of them isn't touching Rick.

Shakily I finish up my beer. "I sh... should be going."

"Don't let me drive you away," says Dan, but it's clear that he doesn't mind if I leave. I struggle up, hoping that there isn't any evidence showing of what has been going on.

"See you," I say in Rick's direction, though that's of course also in Dan's.

I go out into the darkness, trying to analyze my feelings. Am I jealous of Dan? Is he jealous of me? What does Rick feel in this? Was it just a spur of the moment action on his part? Does he do things like that with everybody he can?

Rick is an enigma to me. He's completely different from the sort of person I thought he was, quiet, inhibited, shy – a bit like me – and now I see him quite prepared to wank me off in public, perhaps doing the same with Dan now.

I feel let down though why I should I don't know. Perhaps I wanted Rick all to myself. Oh well, I was wrong, completely wrong. And how am I going to face him on Monday? I trudge down the road between the inadequate village street lamps telling myself I've been a fool to think that I'd find the love of my life so easily.

Suddenly there's the sound of running footsteps behind me. For a moment I wonder whether I'm about to be mugged and almost break into a run, but it's Rick.

"Chris, wait." I stop and turn. We are in the dark area between two street lamps and I can't make out the expression on his face.

"Why did you rush off like that?"

"It was obvious that Dan didn't want me there. I thought you might feel the same."

"Oh Dan. Take no notice of him. He gets funny sometimes."

"He was jealous."

"He has no business to be. We're just friends."

"And you and me?"

There is a pause. I am standing with my back against a house wall. Rick takes a step closer to me. "I hope we're friends. Perhaps we could be something more."

One more step and he's almost touching me. Then he is, his body against mine, his lips on mine. This is worse than being groped in the pub. Anyone could pass and see us. But I don't care. I've never kissed anyone before, not like that anyway. We are touching all the way down and his arms are around me. His tongue forces open my mouth, insinuates itself inside and does things to my body that I've never known before. The kiss goes on for a long time and I can feel the muscles in his chest against mine and further down the hardness of his cock which again equals mine.

Eventually we come up for air. "I want to feel you naked against me," he says. But this is hardly practical in the middle of the village High Street.

There is a burst of raucous singing as a group come out of the pub along the road. Quickly we draw apart.

"Can we go out tomorrow with the dog?"

We walk back to his house together but there are people around so we don't even kiss good-bye.

But there is always tomorrow.

* * *

It's Sunday. I didn't get much sleep last night. My emotions are in a turmoil. I've never felt like this before about anyone, nor indeed experienced anything like what happened yesterday. I'd laid awake thinking about what Rick and I had done – or nearly done – and became aroused. But, perhaps it was stupid, I didn't want to jerk off which probably would have been the best thing, because in some way I wanted to save myself for Rick or is that just stupid?

And again I wondered about Dan. Were he and Rick just 'friends' as Rick had said, and what did that mean? Rick had also said that he and I were 'friends' but that obviously didn't exclude a physical aspect. And had I any right to be jealous of what he and Dan might have done before I knew either of them?

Then I wondered about tomorrow and what would happen. Who would make the first move? Would Rick regret what we had done?

Eventually I must have dropped off to sleep because Mum's bustling around the house wakes me up early. She is a really aggravating person. For months she does little or no housework at all, and then, on a Sunday morning when I could have welcomed a lie in, she starts hoovering at the crack of dawn.

As I come downstairs blearily blinking sleep out of my eyes, she announces that a 'friend' is visiting and she hints that it will be fine by her if I go out, even stay out overnight. There was a time when I used to stay at Dominic's and his friend's Ken Spiller's house but since they've moved away, there's no possibility of that. But I'm not going to admit this and I say, it's okay by me. I wonder if I can possibly stay at Rick's place, though this will be difficult to explain to his parents.

There's a scratch breakfast, a shower, a change of clothes and I'm off to Rick's house. It's obvious that I've arrived in the middle of their breakfast, but his mother doesn't seem put out in the slightest. She dispenses waffles and syrup which I've never had before, but think they're a bloody good substitute for toast and vegetable oil spread, which I can tell from butter.

Rick says we're going out for the day and taking sandwiches and stuff which his mother has prepared. Katie decided that she'd like to come along as well and I hold my breath to see what the result of that is. Rick says it's boys only and she scoffs and mutters, "How gay." But it might just mean in the sense that she disapproves and has no deeper significance. Anyway we ignore her and set off with Sal leaping beside us in utter and abandoned enjoyment.

I'm a little shy after yesterday's passion and my imaginings of last night but once away from the village Rick grabs hold of my hand, turns me round and kisses me.

The rain-washed blue sky is completely cloud free. It is like being on top of the world. I sit on the grass and then I lie back. Rick is lying next to me and the sun cradles us both, sensuously caressing my body and I assume his. I feel my penis hardening and I rearrange it so that it isn't quite so obvious.

I steal a look at my friend lying quietly beside me but Rick's eyes are closed, perhaps he is even asleep. His shirt is rucked up showing his flat stomach and his legs are spread. He looks sprawled and defenseless and I know a moment of complete happiness. I give a quiet sigh, apparently not quiet enough because Rick opens his eyes, looks at me.

And from there he can't help but see the outline of my erection. Rick smiles. "I want to feel you inside me."

"We'll wear each other out."

"What a way to go."

"If we could spend the night together."

"Why not?" Rick asks. "My parents wouldn't mind your sharing my room. And it's got a spare bed in it, which we needn't use."

"My Mum is only too pleased to see the back of me," I remember her last remark to me.

And so it is. Rick's Mum and dad don't seem to find anything strange in my staying overnight. Only Katie gives us an odd look; she's too wily by half for a young girl but there's nothing she can do about it.

We have a scrumptious meal, then watch a bit of television but this is not what we really want so after making an excuse that we are tired after our day out, we go upstairs.

As I go into his room, I gasp with surprise. I know it's a trite cliché but I can't help it. It is like Aladdin's cave. There is a huge 26" plasma screen TV, stereo equipment to fill the Albert Hall with sound (well not quite), latest computer laptop, mobile smart phone with screen which can do practically everything. There's a large bed on one side and a smaller one on the opposite side. I know which one we'll pick.

"Where did you ...?" I ask.

But Rick is suddenly not very communicative. "You know ..." he says, which obviously I don't.

I suspect that he's a bit embarrassed that he's been given all this stuff by his father. I still don't really understand why Rick's got this dead end job but I'm not bothered. There are more important things to think about. Or rather not to think about, just to indulge in.

A Tangled Web

The bed is here, Rick is here, I am here and all three of us need to get together – fast.

Rick slips the lock on the door and we tumble into the bed, that bed so firm, so yielding, just like Rick.

Now I'm not going to describe what happened. Perhaps later when I think about it afterwards. Suffice it to say that we strip each other, revealing our bodies which we cover in … No, that's enough for now.

I am inexperienced but Rick certainly knows his way around and introduces me to all sorts of practices which are so stimulating, occasionally a little painful but in the end so erotic that he has to clamp his hand over my mouth to stop me shouting out.

At last, even we are satisfied and we go to sleep, clasped in each other's arms, even legs entwined and all parts touching. There's nothing I discover so sensual and so comforting as naked skin next to mine.

So, that is how my relationship with Rick starts and proceeds.

* * *

Monday, of course, means back to work and I have to rush home to shower and change ready to be collected by the boss. I don't want to wash Rick off me but I suspect that it's better that I don't get to work smelling of him – or he of me.

I meet Mum's 'visitor', an unshaven guy with a bit of a paunch who doesn't give a toss about me. Why should he? He probably doesn't care much for Mum either, just a casual shag and then off. Is it any different to Rick and me? I think so. I certainly hope so.

No one at work of course suspects and we return to our usual characters, quiet, unassertive and biddable. Occasionally though our eyes meet and we smile knowingly in secret complicity.

Today we are in a grand house on its own and set in a large garden with an orchard at one side. Alterations are to be made, knocking down a wall and building it somewhere else, constructing a conservatory. The owner, a tall thin man with a fruity voice and no chin, points out where everything should be and 'bossman' makes notes though I doubt whether it will make a difference. He knows what he's going to do and that's it. Because they are posh people the owners haven't removed the decorative bits and pieces. There are loads of porcelain statuettes and some pictures. Rick and me are given the task of wrapping these up and storing them away in boxes. I suppose Jas thinks we'll do a good job and not break anything. He does though warn us that they are very valuable and very delicate. No pressure of course!

There are about a hundred of the little horrors, girls in ballet tutus, Victorian ladies with parasols, rather effete young shepherd boys with broad hips and no bulges to speak of where it counts – we giggle a bit over them – each one to be carefully wrapped in newspaper and placed in boxes but, because I'm with Rick, I don't mind the job.

Occasionally 'bossman' pops in to see how we're doing and to hurry us up. Seeing that we're nearly finished he takes me off to help the other lads unload some stuff from a lorry – I've been upgraded.

So that was the day, day three of my affair with Rick – I note them all on my computer, a story in the making, seeing that the tale of Dominic was so inconclusive. I wonder whether I'm too close. Someone once said (I remember it from my English literature lessons at school) that poetry is 'emotion recollected in tranquility' and I guess prose is the same, though I'm anything but tranquil. Even thinking of him gives me a raging hardon and I ache to hold him in my arms again, like we did last night.

At the end of the day, when 'bossman' has dropped us off at our separate houses – I want to go to Rick's but he whispers "later – see you in the pub" and I go home alone.

The man (Mum's 'friend') is still there. Apparently his name is Steve and he's being treated right royally by Mum who has splashed out on a Waitrose 'coq au vin' and raspberry trifle. He must, I think, be a good fuck. I have a couple of slices of pizza but I don't mind.

"We won't be back till late," says Mum. They go out, climb into a not too old Mondeo and roar off. I am alone again. I have a bath, change into some reasonable gear (I'm suddenly envious of Rick's clothes) and set out for the pub. I think of calling in at Rick's house but I don't want to make it too obvious by arriving uninvited – Katie will be bound to make some caustic comment. Anyway, Rick said the pub, so the pub it is.

Of course Dan is behind the bar, blond hair glinting under the lights. My own, mousy brown, needs another visit to the stylist in Chessingham to put back some of the magic that makes me just presentable. Rick, I see because there aren't many people in on a Monday, hasn't arrived yet.

Dan gives me a look which is difficult to interpret. Does he really dislike me? If so will he in fact refuse to serve me because I am underage? I can't hang around waiting for Rick so I go to the bar.

For a moment we stare at each other then I say, "Can I have a beer, please?"

There is another moment of silence and I feel myself going hot. He can so easily ask how old I am and I will blush and stammer as I lie. In fact it will only be a couple of months before my 18th birthday, but those sixty days mean such a lot.

Then Dan says, "Of course you can, sweetie, " and starts to pull me a pint.

From behind I feel a body pushed into me, intimate, familiar. "And one for my friend too," I say without turning round.

But Dan has obviously seen Rick come in for he is already filling a second glass.

We take our drinks to 'our' table and sit as we did on Saturday night, opposite each other, knees touching. I notice that Rick is still wearing his work clothes, a grubby T-shirt with a grey sweat shirt and faded jeans. He hasn't had a bath or shower either and there's a slight smell of sweat. This doesn't upset me. In fact it rather turns me on. I think I prefer the smell of Rick to that of deodorants and soap.

Nevertheless I remark on the fact. "You haven't changed."

"I had to go into Chessingham, and I didn't want to miss you."

I nod, waiting for his explanation of the trip into town but he doesn't say anything more and I don't ask. Instead we talk about other intimate things, things we couldn't mention at work, about our night together and what we did. And how we felt. And how we must do it again.

"And again," I say. "And again."

"You'll get fed up with it."

"Never."

He smiles and feels under the table. I grab his hand and guide it to its target. This, of course was where Dan appeared the last time and I glance across but he's still behind the bar.

Rick works me up into a frenzy until I suddenly say. "This is no good. Let's get out of here and find somewhere where we can do it properly."

As we go out, Dan calls, "Going so soon?" I'm not sure if he's being sarcastic so I ignore him.

Rick waves to him and we leave. Together. My lover and me.

"There's no one at my home." I tell him and I'm too excited to worry about what Rick might think of the state of my house but when we get there and I see the mess, the shabby furniture, the dust which lies on the surfaces – Mum may have cleared up for Steve but her housework isn't of the best – I know Rick must compare it unfavorably with his own house. And my room is, as usual, a complete and utter tip. Even the bed is unmade and books and CDs are littered around as well as, I'm embarrassed to say, some grungy underwear and socks.

I try to kick them surreptitiously under the bed but of course Rick notices. "I'm sorry. I'm a slut."

"And I haven't had a bath. Let's be sluts together."

And indeed we are. I blush at the things we did, and the things we used to do them with. Sometimes the scents and functions of the human body are a complete turn-on and this was one of the times. Even in this, my private writings, I have no intention of telling what we did and how we did it. But it was fucking marvelous and when we finished, sprawled exhausted on a bed which before hadn't been too clean but was now absolutely revolting, I didn't regret it for one moment.

"I think I could do with a shower now," says Rick after a while, and we have one together.

Rick says he has to get back, some family visit. He asks me as well but I decide that I don't want to meet even more of his relatives. We'll meet again tomorrow at work and, after a tender good-bye, he leaves.

* * *

Unfortunately everything goes wrong the following day. When 'bossman' in the van calls, Rick is not aboard. He's been put on some other job, so I'm the 'junior' again, mashing tea and mixing muck. This job is the other side of Chessingham.

"No boyfriend today," says Alf one of the lads, but I ignore him. I expect it's just his idea of a joke.

The day seems longer than ever. Rick and I haven't made any arrangement to meet but he'll either be in the Fag and Fisherman or I could call at his house so I'm not especially worried. We actually finish early so, when Jas gives us a lift back and we pass through Chessingham, I ask to be dropped off there.

"Meeting a bird?" suggests Alf. Really how can he have it both ways?

In fact I've decided to visit the Unisex Hair Salon to have my usual. I'm not embarrassed now and the girl who generally does my hair has become quite a friend. "Same as always, Chris?" she asks, and I nod.

Of course I have to get the bus back but that's no problem and I get to the bus stop with plenty of time to spare. Time indeed to browse some of the shops. There's a clothes shop with a sweat shirt in the window which is like the one Rick has but a different color. I like it but it's way too expensive for me, especially after I've just spent thirty quid having my hair done.

Again I wonder how Rick can afford all the things. Rich dad obviously.

The shop next door is one of those antique ones selling old furniture at incredible prices. Strange when you can get much cheaper stuff from Ikea but I remember how Ken Spiller, Dominic's friend, told me that the old stuff is made with love and attention and lasts much better than the new mass-made things.

On a table in the window are displayed some porcelain figurines, like the ones we were wrapping in that job yesterday. Just out of interest I look at the price tabs. £150 each! Not for the lot! One of them is just the same as the willowy guy Rick and I laughed at, the one with big hips and no cock. If there as common as that I wonder why they're so expensive.

A Tangled Web

There's still ten minutes before the bus is due so I go in and ask the guy in charge why they are so dear. He's a little guy with a bald head and glasses. He sniffs at lot as if he's got a cold or perhaps he's just sniffing out a bargain.

I point to the figurine. "The Goose Boy," he says. "Perfect, isn't it?" He picks it up and rubs it sensuously between his fingers and thumb. Sort of creepy. "It's expensive because it was the only one made." He gestures at the table of statuettes. "They're all one-offs."

"I saw one yesterday exactly the same," I say. "In fact I wrapped it in bubble wrap for the owner."

"Impossible," he says. "Or if you did, it must have been this one. I did in fact only buy it yesterday."

I look at him. "Who from?"

At this he starts to look shifty but comes out with the usual stock phrase. "I'm sorry but I never divulge my sources."

Through the window I can see the bus coming so I run out to catch it.

On the way home I have a lot to think about. If that was the same 'Goose Boy' that we were packing yesterday then someone must have pinched it. Or the owner sold it, but why should he do that? I would have seen if Rick had taken one except that I'd been taken off packing at the end and told to unload the van. And Rick had been to Chessingham yesterday evening before meeting me at the pub. Could he have sold it to the antiques dealer for perhaps £100. £50 is quite a good mark-up profit. Perhaps some of the others are also from the same source. I hadn't paid much attention to the Victorian ladies but I did remember one with a parasol and there was certainly one there like that in the shop.

It feels disloyal to think of Rick as a thief but his possessions and his ready money suggest that he's not living entirely on his wages. Far from it. He can't be earning more than I am and there's no way, I could afford the clothes he wears, the equipment I've seen in his room and his ability to buy drinks in the Fish and Griddle on a regular basis. It must be what his father gives him.

My lover, Rick, a thief? Stealing from the houses he works in and selling them to this dealer? I refuse to believe this. Anyway wouldn't the losses have been noticed? When the builders are in, of course, there's confusion and perhaps a few disappearances could have escaped attention. I argue myself in and out of belief and disbelief. I think it's called playing the Devil's Advocate or something.

Anyway did I even care? As someone who had regularly shoplifted from Woolworth's in my youth I can't claim that I was as driven snow as regards crime. But those thefts were really to prove I was one of the lads and I'd never thought of doing it for profit, just for street credibility.

If Rick had embarked on a life of crime, could he be trusted in other matters? Clearly I'm confused. I could ask him, of course, but do I want to drag it into the open? Do I want to show him that I don't think of him as anything but my glorious, sexy lover?

So perturbed am I that I nearly miss my stop but get off just in time. Steve is still in residence and Mum looks happier than she has done for years. She doesn't snap at me, and I'm included in the dinner arrangements which, for a change, are not 'chips with everything'.

I'd have said yesterday that my sexual adventures have given me a sunnier personality. Today I'm not so sure.

As soon as I can, though, I escape by offering to do the washing up, and then I'm off. I call at Rick's but Katie informs me, with a note of glee in her voice – or am I being too sensitive? – that he isn't in and she doesn't know where he is.

I go to the pub but he isn't there either. And nor is Dan behind the bar. I ask the barman who is on duty where Dan is and he rather grudgingly tells me it's his night off. There's no point in my staying here so I go home in a state of mingled jealousy (are the two of them out together?) and worry. I really am a complete prick sometimes. In extenuating of course I've never been in love before with its alternate highs and lows.

I try to watch some telly but there's nothing of interest on the five terrestrial channels (we don't have Sky). I write a bit on the computer putting down my thoughts but it just makes me more miserable. Where is Rick?

Towards eleven o'clock, Mum and Steve come in. An early night for them but perhaps they want to go to bed. At their age. Gross! Mum starts fiddling around in the kitchen and I realize that I haven't eaten anything since a pie at lunchtime. Often she brings back a Chinese or Indian but tonight she's doing the Jamie Oliver – beans on toast! And she even does one for me. I take a bite but suddenly find I've lost my appetite. I don't want to cause a row so I battle on manfully.

Then the phone rings. Mum says, "Who on earth can be ringing at this time of night?"

Steve grunts – his usual form of communication. Mum picks up the receiver, listens and then says to me, "It's for you."

Speed of light across the room. Even Steve is moved to comment. "Must be the girl friend."

Mum says, "It was a bloke."

And Steve grunts again.

But I don't care. "Hello."

A muffled voice says, "It's Rick." I nearly blurt out what I feel, how glad I am to hear from him, that I love him, that I want to see him immediately, touch him, kiss him – and all the etceteras that that implies. But I force myself to be calm.

"Missed you today."

"Sorry," he says, his voice sounding a bit strained and strange. "There were problems."

"What sort of problems?"

"Can you speak?"

I look round at Mum and Steve who are attending closely. "Not really."

"Can we meet?"

"Now?"

"Yes. I'll wait outside the church." He rings off.

"Gotta go out," I say. "Important."

"Not getting yourself into trouble, are you?" asks Mum.

"More like getting someone else in trouble," is Steve's comment.

I ignore them both and make for the door. Insanely I am singing to myself 'Get me to the church on time'.

It is dark. Of course it's dark. It is nearly midnight but I mean dark, dark. The street lights have been turned off and there's only a trace of a moon, smiling on its side through a break in the clouds. Soon though I get accustomed and can make out the dark shapes of buildings, with the occasional lighted window.

The church is a great slab of blackness against the grey sky with a tall tower at one end. I can't see anyone waiting there but as I get close a shadow steps out from under the lych gate.

"Rick?" Who else can it be?

But it isn't. The figure isn't right. Too tall. As he gets close, the hair isn't right. Too light. He grabs me around the chest imprisoning my arms. He's strong, and though I struggle, I can't get free. His smell is wrong too. Not Rick's at all. A pungent, acrid smell, fear and anger combined.

His mouth is close to my ear. "Nosy little fucker," he snarls.

I know who it is then. "Dan!"

He holds me with one arm and even that is strong enough to keep me against his body. His other hand snakes down and grabs hold of my balls. He squeezes and I scream with the pain, doubling up and falling to the ground. He follows me down, lying across me. I can smell him even stronger and still his hand doesn't leave go.

He is whispering vicious, venomous words. "Asking questions, you little shit. Not minding your own business. If you ever want to come again, you'll forget everything you've been poking your nose into. Understand?"

I am past being able to speak. I nod even though I don't understand.

He gives another agonizing squeeze. I feel sick with the pain which has spread from my groin through the whole of my body. "Understand?"

It is all I can do to grunt out a 'yes', and he relaxes his grip.

I am crying and I lie on the ground curled up, moaning.

He moves away but then returns and kicks me in the ribs. "Forget everything," he repeats.

I don't need telling again. It's difficult to think when I'm in such agony, and only another male can know the pain that crushed testicles can produce but as I slowly get up and hobble, bent double towards home I work out the possibilities.

The only thing I can think of is the odd affair in the Chessingham antique shop. Could it be that the antique dealer I visited and 'interrogated' in Chessingham has told Dan that someone is on to him, presumably described me and Dan has decided to frighten me off. No problem there. I thought he was going to kill me.

But the real doubt I have, when the pain allows me to even a modicum of thought is whether Dan and Rick are in this together. In that case I've been well and truly shafted by someone I trusted, indeed thought I was in love with, and that caused more pain than my poor mistreated balls.

I am glad that Mum and Steve have gone to bed when I get in. They'd surely have commented on how I crawl so painfully up the stairs and into bed. Not that I get much sleep. I wonder if I am terminally damaged, and also whether my heart as well as my testicles are broken.

* * *

Next morning I plead sickness and ask Mum to tell bossman that I won't be working today. I hear her doing just that and also hear Jas grumbling about how it's impossible to rely on workmen these days and whether he wouldn't be better to employ Polish or East European workers who are much more reliable. He's also having a shout at someone else but I bury my head in the pillow and try and shut out the outside world – for ever.

A little later I hear the bedroom door open and assume that it's Mum who, out of the goodness of her heart, has brought me up a cup of tea or at least a grilling as to what is really wrong with me or if I'm just being a lazy wanker.

"Not now, Mum."

A voice says, "Chris."

I peer out from under the covers. In the doorway is Rick. Christ! I must look a mess, eyes, red-rimmed, hair all over the place, ears no doubt sticking out like jug-handles. Does it even matter now?

He comes in and sits down on the bed. "Chris, I'm so sorry," he says.

Sorry for what? Sorry for setting Dan on me? Sorry for being in with Dan and just using me as a temporary fuck? The thoughts jumble in that tiny part of my brain that is able to think of anything but my balls.

He touches my cheek with the palm of his hand. This tenderness is too much for me. I start to cry. He bends his head and kisses the tears that are rolling down my cheeks.

"It wasn't me," he says. "I didn't steal anything. Just talked about the stuff to Dan. He did the breaking in and pinched those porcelain bits and pieces. I knew he was doing it but thought he was my friend. I couldn't shop him."

"All that money you had," I say. "I thought it was you, stealing and selling the stuff."

"Just gifts from my Dad. I was embarrassed to admit it. He's generous with his money, both to me and to Katie."

"Did you know Dan was going to do that to me. I thought he was going to kill me."

"Of course I didn't. I didn't get home until late. We were all questioned by the police. They didn't let us go until really late. Dan told me what he'd done to you. Sounded pleased with himself. 'Scared the shit our of the little fucker,' he said."

"He was right."

"It's all over between Dan and me." Rick lies down beside me and tenderly holds my face in his hands, kissing me gently on the lips.

I want to push myself against him but it's too painful. I am getting the beginnings of an erection though which is a good sign. Perhaps I've not been permanently damaged.

I hope I can trust Rick. I want to – but Christ, life is so fucking complicated innit?.

Chapter 4 Life on the Verge

I thought long and hard about Rick. Rick who was my boyfriend, my lover, my partner – wasn't he? I hadn't been out long, only recently admitted to myself that I was gay and moreover had only just entered into this, my first relationship with someone else.

I was insecure. I felt I needed constant reassurance and then told myself that I shouldn't be such a bloody fool. Rick and I had been together for, what was it? More than six months now, seeing each other as much as we could, and, at least as far as I was concerned, always feeling that same excitement when a meeting was imminent, and the same pleasurable jab in the solar plexus when I caught sight of Rick, opening the door, coming round a corner of the road, seeing him sitting waiting in the corner of the pub.

I didn't want to appear clingy or always demanding loyalty/support or proof of affection so I attempted a light-hearted approach to the relationship. Much as I wanted to, I wouldn't rush into the arms of my beloved, nor demand professions of undying love and consequently when I never got them, I worried.

The vicious attack by a jealous ex of Rick's had left me with a lack of certainty about whether the relationship with Rick would succeed or indeed last for any length of time. My self-confidence/self-esteem had never been very high mostly because of the poor opinions and negative attitude of my mother.

Now, Rick had moved on to another job, more money, more interest, better prospects. I was pleased for Rick's sake but upset, no that was too weak a word, almost devastated by the fact that I wouldn't see Rick on a daily basis.

We had of course discussed the change, at length and often.

"Chris, do you think I should take this new job?" Rick had asked. "My dad pulled lots of strings to get it for me." Rick's father, unlike mine who had fled the family when I was only fifteen, was supportive and in fact spoiled his son 'something rotten' (as I thought of it).

"Of course you must," I had said stoutly though every fibre of my being argued against the move. "You'd be a fool not to."

"We won't be able to see as much of each other."

"Stop us getting fed up," I said.

"You may be right." Now why, I thought didn't Rick say something like 'we'll never get tired of each other'.

So Rick started on his career as an apprentice in an engineering firm and I missed his daily presence. I could also envisage Rick growing further and further away as his job prospects increased. What would a fully fledged engineer want with a builder's assistant/plaster mixer?

But we still saw each other most evenings. I would go round to Rick's house where Mrs Harrison always made me welcome so unlike my own mother who treated me more as an encumbrance, someone who got in the way of her latest 'friend', a burly electrician called Steve.

Rick had described his mother as 'weird', though I decided that, if she was, I liked her brand of weirdness. She was a staunch supporter of homeopathic medicines, that strange belief that the essence of a drug though diluted so much that scarcely a molecule of the original substance still remained, somehow imprints its memory on the liquid so that it was effective in curing all sorts of diseases. Or at least that's what Mrs Harrison explained. I couldn't see it, but, as long as she didn't want to cure something serious with her medicines, she was welcome to her beliefs.

She always accepted my arrival as if it was the most natural thing in the world and treated me almost as another son. Rick's dad also seemed to like me. Only Katie, Rick's younger sister, occasionally looked askance at the closeness of the bond between her brother and this 'visitor', especially as, when it occasionally happened, I stayed overnight and the two of us shared the same room. Admittedly there were two beds but Katie on one occasion had been discovered checking them to see if both had been slept in. They hadn't though Rick and I had ruffled the bedclothes to make it appear that they had.

One evening in December I went round to find that Rick wasn't at home. "Never mind, dear," said Mrs Harrison. "He'll be back later but apparently they had to go down to Southampton on some day course and he won't be back until late."

I wondered why I hadn't been told and started to make my excuses and return home.

"Don't go, Chris," said Mrs Harrison. "Stay for some supper, but first you can come with me to my meeting. Rick will surely be back by the time we return."

"Meeting?"

Mrs Harrison smiled. "Yes, dear. A Spiritualist Meeting. You'll enjoy it. The medium's a dear old lady but she's very good. Gets messages from everywhere, people who have crossed the Great Divide."

I wasn't too keen on the idea. I had long ago decided there was no god, certainly not a merciful, beneficent one who allowed such injustices and cruelty to innocents in the world.

The alternative though was an evening with Steve and Mum, or staying with Katie who gave the excuse that she had homework to do and, much though she'd like to attend the Meeting, it wasn't really possible. She gave me a knowing look and raised an eyebrow as if to say, 'I can find my own excuses. You do what you can.'

Apart from saying I didn't want to go, I could think of no valid excuse. I went.

The Meeting was held in the old Baptist chapel Hall, a long low drafty building with insufficient heating especially on a cold December night like this. It smelled of antiseptic and old hymn books. The chairs were hard and uncomfortable and the little, white-haired old lady, Mrs Florence Cook, whom I was introduced to and who shook my hand with a frail hand of her own that felt as if it could easily be crushed, didn't give me much expectation of excitement.

I wondered if there would be clouds of ectoplasm or ghosts appearing? Mrs Harrison, to whom I whispered my question said, she doubted it but you never knew.

The lights were low wattage anyway but when half of them were switched off it was almost too dim to see much. However there was one bulb over Mrs Cook which shone on her hair making it appear like a white halo and hiding her features.

I was skeptical in the extreme, a view that the opening prayer, chanted by the audience, who were obviously regulars, did nothing to dispel. It seemed to call on the powers of the dead to appear especially any which had special messages for members of the congregation.

"Sometimes, when they come," whispered Mrs Harrison, "the room gets very cold."

I wasn't sure how they'd tell. It was freezing enough anyway. I sat obediently though and wished the whole thing would be over soon, so that we could return to a nice, warm house and the arms of my beloved.

Suddenly Mrs Cook spoke, her voice sounding much stronger and deeper than it had when she'd greeted me at first. 'Good actress,' I thought.

"Is there anyone here called Rose?"

A woman in the audience held up her hand.

"I have a message for you from your husband, who has recently passed over. He tells you not to be downhearted, that he is safely in the Hereafter and you will both meet up again in due course."

'Oh yes,' I thought. 'A nice, bland message it'll come a cropper if her husband is actually at home looking after the kids. Perhaps, though, Mrs Cook had done her homework, for Rose subsided looking pleased.'

Then Mrs Cook spoke again. "Is there anyone here called Chris?"

I started, then said to myself. She knows there is. We have just been introduced.

Mrs Harrison dug me in the ribs with her elbow. "Say you're here," she said.

It was rubbish and I felt a bit of a fool but I obeyed. "I'm Chris."

"There is a message for you from someone called Ken."

My first thought was that I didn't know anyone named Ken, but then with a sudden shock I realized that I did. I remembered Kenneth Spiller, the author I had met some months before, the one who had gone off to live with Dominic in the little border town of Hay on Wye.

But Kenneth Spiller wasn't dead, was he? Admittedly I hadn't heard of or from him since the parting some six months before. Spiller wasn't all that old and had seemed in perfectly sound health, apart from his leg which had been injured some years earlier.

Mrs Cook was continuing speaking. "Ken wants to say that someone close to you will let you down. There is a warning of desertion."

She turned to someone else. "Is there anyone here named Sadie?" she asked.

I was left in a whirl of conflicting emotions. Part of me wanted to say that the whole thing was absolute rubbish. The old lady had known I was in the audience, perhaps realized I was impressionable. The message wasn't specific enough to need any particular knowledge, except for the name, Ken. Ken dead? And who was this person who was going to desert me? If there was anything in this spiritualist stuff then surely it could only be Rick. But Rick wouldn't do anything like that. Would he? And if it was him, how would Kenneth, who had never met him, know?

I wanted to get out as quickly as possible but there was no way I could leave without barging through the audience and drawing attention to myself. I had to sit while the old hag up there went through this list of people and passed on banal messages, some possibly of comfort, others of censure or foreboding, until with a sigh of relief the farce was over and we escaped.

Mrs Harrison, though, didn't seem to be much concerned. On the contrary, the fact that I had been picked out for special mention seemed almost a triumph for her.

"Fancy you having a message, on your first time too." She didn't seem to bother that someone close to me was going to desert me. I, who had always been worried that this might happen, and especially since Rick had started on his new career, was cast further into depression.

It was in low spirits, therefore, that I returned to the Harrison house to find that Rick still hadn't arrived and, though both Mr and Mrs Harrison pressed me to stay for a meal, I found I had lost my appetite and prepared to go home.

I was in fact just on the doorstep when the phone rang.

"Hang on," said Mr Harrison. "This may be him."

It was.

The coach bringing the apprentices back from Southampton had broken down in a dead spot where there was no mobile phone signal, so he'd been unable to tell us earlier. However they wouldn't be able to get back home that evening and would stay the night at an hotel in the New Forest. Rick didn't sound disappointed. In fact he made it sound like an adventure and one which he was enjoying.

"See you soon," he said airily and broke the connection.

I was disappointed. I again refused the offer of a meal and went home where all I could find to eat was a day old piece of pizza in the fridge which I ate, accompanied by the sounds of Mum and Steve having sex in the front bedroom. These rather grim noises, creaking springs, harsh breathing (presumably Steve) and little squeaks (probably Mum) or it might have been the other way round, doing little to cheer me up.

The message from Mrs Cook was obviously utter drivel but at least Rick could have sounded more disappointed at not being able to meet up with me. I worried about it during the night, waking up two or three times and then not being able to doze off again immediately so that I overslept in the morning and it was only when bossman, Jas, sounded the horn outside the house in the morning that I awoke. I had no time to do anything else but struggle into my T-shirt and jeans, socks and trainers, have a piss and grab my jacket.

Jas grumbled at having to wait, but that was nothing new.

My stomach rumbled uncomfortably all the way to the job site. I realized that I had had hardly any food since the day before morning and the ride was long – Hereford being some forty miles from Elmcombe – so that I felt slightly sick when we arrived. That would indeed have been adding insult to injury if I'd thrown up in the van on the way.

Luckily, Jas always had his priorities. "Put the kettle on, Chrissy," he said and with a cup of tea inside me, and a bacon sarnie from the shop down the road, I would feel better.

I wondered what Rick was doing, presumably not acting as 'tea boy' and fetcher of the sandwiches for the rest of the group. 'See you soon', he'd said but when?

It was when I was at the shop that a road sign caught my eye. It indicated that the road ahead led to Hay on Wye, 27 miles. This, of course brought all the thoughts and worries of yesterday back to me. Twenty seven miles. It wasn't far but to me who had no form of transport except a rickety bicycle back in Elmcombe, it was as distant as Timbuktu.

At the job site I was hanging around doing very little and waiting for someone to demand some more plaster be made up when the owner of the house drifted in. He was a mild-mannered man with glasses and a failed comb-over.

"I suppose none of you young men know your way round a computer," he said.

Jas, who liked to help out customers, especially when it didn't cause him personally any work, said, "Chrissy, you've got one. See if you can help the gentleman."

I had my extremely old word processor, donated to me by Kenneth Spiller when he had left Elmcombe, the same Kenneth whom I now wondered if he was dead, was about to protest. But I had, in the course of my somewhat intermittent school attendance, been to quite a few I.T. classes (more interesting than Maths or French) and thought I might be able to answer at least simple questions.

It was indeed a simple problem. "I'm looking for suppliers of certain goods," the man told me. This was inexact but perhaps he had his reasons.

"No problem," I said. "All you need is to put what you want into a search engine - as long as you've got access to the Internet."

The man looked vague, but it happened that he had, so I pulled one up, and then had an idea. I told him, "Suppose I want to search for Bookshops in Hay on Wye," I said. "I'd put in 'Bookshops' and "Hay on Wye". I did so and clicked on 'Search'. Almost immediately I was told that there were about 23,000 sites answering to this description. I clicked on the first and a list of bookshops appeared. Almost forgetting that I was supposed to be helping the old gent, I skimmed down the list. It wasn't in alphabetical order, never is, but looking down the first page I found the entry: Dominic Spiller, rare books and the phone number.

I made a mental note of this and then turned. "See how easy it is."

The man was impressed. "I usually get the wife to do the computer work but this one I can do on my own."

I hung around to see if he needed any more help, but it appeared that the man didn't really want an audience for whatever it was he was looking for so I left.

Why Dominic had taken Kenneth's surname, I had no idea. Was it something to do with Ken's death, if he had actually died? I'd ring up and find out as soon as I could. In the meantime, I found a pencil and wrote down the number before I forgot it. I had my own cell phone, a primitive affair but prohibited by Jas in case those with more modern smart phones might waste their time, playing games or looking at porn sites.

That evening I again went round to Rick's house. Rick still wasn't there. "He's been back earlier today," said Mrs Harrison, "but he said he had to go out again."

"Did he leave me a message?"

"'Fraid not, dear. He was excited about something though he didn't say what. I expect he'll be in touch later this evening."

But no phone call came and, alone in my house, for Mum and Steve had gone out, I waited, and waited, and waited and no shrilling of the telephone disturbed the silence of the house.

You know what it's like when you're expecting a call, especially a call from someone special, and it doesn't come, you start to imagine all sorts of dreadful things, accidents, deliberate snubs, desertion. I felt all of these, but my pride wouldn't allow me to ring up the Harrisons. If Rick didn't want to get in touch, then I wouldn't go a-begging. But I felt sick with disappointment and worry and frustration.

Eventually, rather than going mad I decided to ring the Hay on Wye number. If it was just a shop there wouldn't be anyone there at this time of night but perhaps they lived there. I could imagine Kenneth living in a room surrounded by books, the smell of dusty old volumes in the air but a smell that Spiller would love. I couldn't exactly picture Dominic in such surroundings. I remembered the both of us, running through the countryside with the collie dog Shannon at our sides.

I dialed the number and then, suddenly losing my bottle, I put the phone down again as soon as it started ringing at the other end. Then, calling myself a stupid coward, I reached out my hand for the phone again when it rang.

My heart missed a beat. It must be Rick after all. I grabbed the receiver and said, "Hello. About time too."

But it wasn't Rick's voice at the other end.

"Is that Chris?"

"Yes, Who is it?"

"Dominic."

Confused I said, "I was just going to ring you."

"You did already, and then rang off before I could answer. Your number was displayed on my phone and, although I didn't recognize it, I wondered if it might be you. How are you?"

I didn't know what to say. How was I? Confused? Upset? Why in fact had I wanted to get in touch with Dominic. Then I remembered. "How's Ken?" I asked.

"I'll tell you when we meet. You do want to meet don't you? It would be good to see you again. I've often wondered what's been happening to you."

"It's difficult to get over to Hay. It was just that I'm working at Hereford and saw a signpost."

"There's a bus from Hereford to Hay. Or if you tell me the time you finish work, I can come over in the car and fetch you."

Things were slipping out of my grasp. What was I letting myself in for? Almost in a panic, I said, "But how will I get back?"

"Do you have to?"

I could imagine what Dominic would look like. Sitting in an armchair holding the phone. Dark hair cut short, a smile revealing white teeth. When I'd last seen him, his face and body tanned by the Mediterranean sun after his Greek holiday.

I had never been one for the sudden, impulsive decision but I made one now. "I'd like that. Is it okay if I ring you when we finish work tomorrow? Won't you be working though?"

"Self-employed," said Dominic. "I can shut up shop any time I like."

We left it like that.

I wondered whether I ought to tell Rick that I might not be available the following evening. I didn't exactly feel guilty because nothing was going to happen, and why shouldn't I meet an old friend whom I hadn't seen for some time. Rick after all had left me in the lurch for the past two days without even an explanation of what he was doing, or even where he was.

If Rick phoned, I would tell him of course but there was no phone call and I went to bed and slept reasonably well. After all I'd had a sleepless night the night before. I was disturbed when Mum and Steve got back but soon dropped off again. I dreamed of Rick, or was it Rick? Could it have been

Dominic? Anyway it was a wildly erotic dream and in it I was rolling around in a bed with some incredibly sexy person.

I didn't oversleep and was ready when Jas and the boys arrived. Leaving via the hall, I suddenly noticed that the telephone receiver was off the hook. Had Mum taken it off so that she and Steve wouldn't have been disturbed? If Rick had phoned, he wouldn't have been able to get through but it was too late to worry about that now and I didn't want to share my private calls in the van using my (forbidden but hidden) mobile. By the time we reached Hereford, Rick would have left for work so I'd have to wait until the evening.

When work ended, I told Jas I wouldn't need taking home. I was seeing a friend who would pick me up and bring me back in the morning. "Found a rich boyfriend?" suggested Alf but there was no malice in his tone and they all laughed.

As the van disappeared, I had a moment's panic when I wondered if Dominic, for some reason, wouldn't be able to fetch me and I'd be left alone in the middle of nowhere with no means of getting home, but Dominic answered the mobile immediately and said he'd be there in half an hour at the latest.

I hoped he wouldn't be any longer. It was a cold though clear December evening and, though the street lamps were on, they weren't bright enough to hide the stars appearing overhead together with half a waxing moon. In the bus shelter which was where I had arranged to meet Dominic, I rang Rick but only the answer phone responded.

I left no message.

The car, a Ford Mustang, drew up just when I was starting to worry. Dominic leant out of the window. "You must be frozen, Chris," he said. "Hop in." He looked no different to what he had done when I saw him last, dark, good-looking, a ready smile, qualities that always made me feel inferior – yet it was he who had called me 'cute' that time on the hill when we had first walked the dog, Shannon. And something had happened, or nearly happened.

The car heater was on and it was comfortably warm inside. Dominic leant across and planted a kiss on my cheek. I was surprised but far from upset. We started out into the night and soon left Hereford behind. I decided I'd have to find out what I needed to know. After all the whole thing depended on Mrs Cook's assertion that Kenneth was dead and from the after life had warned that I would be deserted by someone close to me. Certainly Rick's behavior over the last few days had implanted suspicions and doubts about his faithfulness.

But how to put it? I tried a neutral question. "How's Kenneth?" I had asked this before over the phone and then had not got an answer.

There was a silence and I was sure that this time the answer would be that Dominic's partner had died. But then Dominic said, "Surely you came to see me, not Kenneth."

Another evasion. "You both were very kind to me," I said, "when I was feeling very low. Of course I'm pleased to see you but Kenneth started me on this writing business and ..."

"How's the writing going?"

I hadn't written anything really since my affair with Rick had started, so I was non committal. "Okay," I said vaguely. And to change the subject, I asked, "And how's the book business?"

Dominic launched into an account of how it was quite lucrative, how the business was flourishing (hence the Mustang) and what the International Book Week meant for individual book shops. There'd been the usual winter weekend Festival with visiting authors, book signings and all the paraphernalia of a literary shindig.

Soon we were in Hay and drew up outside a double fronted shop with what looked like Tudor beams and a sign saying 'Dominic Spiller – Antiquarian and Second-hand Books'. Dominic unlocked the shop door, switched on some lights and led the way through aisles of bookshelves to the back where there was a flight of stairs and at the top a door.

The room immediately inside the door had a sofa and an easy chair, a pine table under the window, a music center and a TV set with video. Book shelves held books of the sort that I knew must have been chosen by Kenneth, but there were no other signs of him. A cabinet with drawers against the wall had some bottles and glasses standing on top. A door in one corner led off to a kitchen, there were others shut which presumably led to bedrooms and a bathroom. Several rugs spread scarlet patches over the floor and some pictures, framed views of sea coasts, hung on the walls. An appetizing smell of something cooking made my taste buds drool.

Dominic took off his jacket. Unexpectedly uneasy, I stood uncertain what to do next.

"Now for some food. It's been cooking all afternoon. Hungry?"

"You bet. Ravenous."

Dominic switched on the television and went into the kitchen. "Sit down," he said through the doorway. "Make yourself comfortable."

I considered the easy chair, then chose the sofa. The TV set picture showed the news. It wasn't particularly interesting and I picked up a paperback which was lying open, face down on the table behind. It was an American crime story by someone I had never heard of. There was a picture of a man in a broad-brimmed hat on the cover. Hardly Ken's choice.

I realized that I still hadn't settled the problem of Ken. I decided finally to come out with it. "Where's Ken?"

The answer was unexpected. "Leeds," Dominic said. "There's a house clearance there with, it's rumored some pretty interesting books. You can't keep Ken away from things like that."

Ken wasn't dead! Mrs Cook had made the whole thing up or at least had deluded herself with her 'messages from the other side'. Which meant that the information which I had decided referred to Rick probably wasn't true either. Yet Rick's behavior over the last few days had given me the distinct impression that there was something wrong, our relationship was turning sour.

"Food, glorious food," said Dominic, bringing in two steaming plates.

The meal - a slowly cooked moussaka, layers of minced lamb, aubergines, tomatoes, topped with a creamy cheese sauce served with a green salad and a bottle of white wine - tasted delicious.

"I didn't know you were such a good cook."

"It's the only thing I can make."

To complement the Greek dish, Dominic admitted to having bought some baklava from the local delicatessen, a sweet pastry with nuts, dripping with honey. He made the coffee while I gobbled up the dessert.

Afterwards we sat on the sofa, side by side. "It's good to see you after so long," said Dominic. "I've thought about you a lot."

I wondered if I could say the same. If I were honest, since Ken and Dominic had left Elmcombe for Hay, my thoughts had been elsewhere and centered on Rick.

"I've missed you too," I said, and it wasn't entirely a lie, just something that I hadn't admitted to myself.

Dominic put his arm round my shoulders in what I assumed was a comradely gesture. I turned to face him and our lips met. Then Dominic was kissing me with a fervor which was far from 'comradely'. I smelled his scent, a mixture of after shave and 'young man'. I remembered it from the last time, when we had wrestled together on the hill above Elmcombe. At the same time his free hand was in my' groin feeling for, and finding my cock through the layers of clothing.

To say I didn't react would be a lie. Although I had only recently admitted to myself that I was gay, I was as ready as any other healthy gay man to get excited when an attractive guy sticks his tongue in my mouth, has his body pressed next to me and holds my cock in his hand.

I did manage though to let common sense prevail. "This is making things more complicated," I said as well as I could when my mouth was full of tongue and more than anything I wanted that hand to go inside my trousers, and perform skin to skin.

Then it was as if I had unzipped my trousers and invited Dominic inside. Anyway that's where his hand went and his mouth fastened on to mine like a lamprey, his tongue forcing my lips, teeth open and roving around inside until I felt that a tonsillectomy was imminent.

Parts of me (my cock in particular) seemed to take on a life of their own when groped by questing fingers. "No. No," I attempted to say though my mouth was full of probing muscle. "Yes. Yes," said my cock rising to its full extent.

But there were no excuses for what I did and allowed Dominic to continue doing. I knew I'd feel guilty afterwards but that didn't stop me putting my hand onto Dominic's groin, feeling, through the material, the softness of scrotum and balls, and then a hardening shape. Dominic breathed deeply and I grasped hold of his cock, using my other hand to find and draw down his zip. Inside, the softness of underwear. I pushed Dominic's trousers down to his knees. I felt Dominic's hands on the back of my head drawing me down towards Dominic's groin and I could smell the exciting scent of man, see the outlined shape obviously impatient to be out of the confines of his briefs.

I obliged and took it out, feeling the soft silkiness of the surface skin surrounding the hard stem. I kiss-licked the top, prepared to take the whole thing into my mouth when –

There were sounds from below and feet clumped up the stairs in a heavy limping rhythm.

A voice, Kenneth's voice, called, "Dom, I'm back."

"Shit," Dominic said and stood up hastily.

Frantic adjustment of cocks and underwear and doing up of zip fasteners. Dominic slipped back into the armchair and I looked – I hoped – composed.

"Come in, Kenneth," said Dominic. "We have a visitor."

It was a classic situation. The guilty pair discovered in flagrante. But Kenneth Spiller looked anything but angry. He smiled with such innocent enjoyment when he saw me that I felt guilty thinking of what so nearly had happened. I thought he looked younger than ever in spite of the greying hair. Obviously living in the book world with Dominic suited him.

Explanations followed, how I had been working in Hereford. How seeing the road sign to Hay had reminded me of the two of them (Accent on the 'two' which in a way was true). How searching the Internet for the owner of the house we were working on had brought up the telephone number and how Dominic had invited me over for a meal.

"Excellent," said Kenneth, "And has he fed you well?"

"Delicious moussaka."

"Ah, the only thing he knows how to make."

"How was the house clearance?" asked Dominic.

"Disappointing! Which is why I'm back so early. There was nothing of any real value."

"Ken thinks that nothing published after 1850 is worthy of his attention. I try to convince him otherwise but you know how old people get set in their ways."

Ken laughed. Clearly he and Dominic had reached a stage in their relationship where teasing was given and accepted in good grace. I thought I envied them, but then wondered about what had so nearly happened. What did that say about the relationship? And what, I asked myself, did it say about mine and Rick's possibly already shaky one?

There was no time to think about that for Ken was asking me about my own life since we had parted, then insisted on showing me some of the 'treasures' that he had managed to acquire since coming to Hay.

Suddenly I remembered. "Where's Shannon?" I asked, having a liking for the affectionate collie which had brought the three of us together after the disastrous flood which had ruined Ken's cottage. "And Princess," I added remembering the cat.

"They're still here, or at least with my parents at the moment."

"We can take Shannon for a walk tomorrow morning if you like," Dominic said. "I can still get you to work in time."

I stayed the night in the spare room (or so they called it). It was a bit like a cupboard with a narrow single bed in it and piles of books all around. In fact they had to clear the bed before it could be made up for me. I guess Dominic had been planning on both of us sharing the main bed before Kenneth had made his unexpected appearance.

I was confused, to say the least. I felt I had let down Kenneth, let down Rick (though this wasn't quite confirmed. I didn't know what he had been doing or indeed what the situation was between us). I must admit I didn't sleep all that well and the fact that the bed wasn't particularly comfortable wasn't the only reason. Why on earth, I wondered, had I believed some crackpot old woman whom I'd now proved to be wrong?

At six o'clock I was awake and up and Dominic and Ken were making toast and coffee. It was still dark but Dominic and I collected Shannon. I had wondered whether the dog would remember me but I needn't have worried. With an excited yelp she flung herself at me, jumping up and trying to lick my face, then lying on her back so that I could stroke her stomach. Typical dog! Princess, the cat, was much less effusive but I think she did remember me. Dominic's parents, he said, were not yet up.

We set out with a torch but it wasn't really necessary. It was one of those cold winter mornings, when the temperature was way below freezing, the grass was white with frost crystals and the stars and the half moon provided all the light that was needed. We had to walk quickly just to keep the blood circulating and there was no question of our stopping for anything physical, but Dominic put his hand in my jeans pocket and I in his and we went along together, Shannon gamboling gleefully beside us.

We didn't talk much. I wanted to ask him about his relationship with Ken but thought that would be too intrusive and he didn't volunteer any information. The silence, though, was comradely and not embarrassing. On the way back, Dominic stopped and kissed me just once.

"It's good to see you," he said. "And Kenneth told me that he hopes you're getting on okay with everything."

I would have liked to have been able to say that everything was fine, that I had a lover, that we been fucking like rabbits at every available opportunity and that I was the happiest guy alive but ... Instead I just said "I'm okay."

And he said "We must keep in touch," and then he drove me back to Hereford talking about other things and arriving just as Jas unloaded the crew.

"At least you're on time," said Jas typically.

"New boyfriend?" asked Alf.

"Old acquaintance," I snapped, shutting him up. "At least I've got friends."

It had been three days since I'd seen Rick and two since I'd even talked to him. I was dreading actually making contact after last night's fiasco but I did ring the Harrisons when I had a spare moment and wasn't surrounded by the gang and Alf's flapping ears.

Mrs Harrison was home. "Rick's been trying to contact you," she said. "He said it's most urgent but you haven't been at home and apparently your mobile's switched off."

It had been. Getting calls at work was prohibited by Jas and anyway Alf was too curious by half.

"Did he say what he wanted?"

"No, dear, but he did say it was very important."

"I'll call round this evening."

Heart thumping and wondering if my peccadilloes would actually show like some dreadful spreading leprosy over visible parts of my body I called round. Actually I'd been home first but neither Mum nor Steve were in so I had a shower, hoping this would wash away my sins.

Rick opened the door. I stood and looked at him for a moment almost as if he was a stranger. Then, breaking all my rules I stepped forward, enclosed him in a bear hug and kissed him. I expected, hoped for a similar response but I what I got shocked me. He pulled back and a voice from behind explained the reason.

"I always knew you two were gay," said Katie from the shadows in the hall.

"We'll tell Mum and Dad in due course," said Rick. "You just mind your own business."

"Expect they know already," said the dreadful child, "from the way you're always carrying on."

"Come upstairs," said Rick.

He took my hand and dragged me in. As we passed the kitchen, Mrs Harrison's called out, "Is that you, Chris? Special meal tonight. Hope you're hungry."

"Down in a minute, Mum."

Once in his room, he pulled me to him. "Where have you been? I've been ringing and ringing."

"Same here, but you were never at home."

"What about last night?"

"I was staying with a couple of friends in Hay on Wye. I told you about them once. Booksellers."

Rick nodded and then we spent a bit of time doing what came naturally.

"I thought you'd gone off me." It sounded wimpish when I said it but I didn't care. "When you went off to Southampton and then didn't seem to want to see me."

"You prat. You fucking prat. Do you know what I've been doing these past few days? Apart from worrying about you of course."

"So what have you been doing?" I was glad he wasn't asking me as I'm sure I'd have started blushing when I thought about what had nearly happened with Dominic the previous night.

"It's time I stopped living at home. I've been looking around for a flat. Of course I'd need someone to share it with. I'd like it to be you."

I was dumbfounded. The objections seemed immense. I struggled to put them into words. "But ... how could we afford it? You're only an apprentice and I'm on minimum wage."

"That's no problem. Dad's agreed to buy it for us and we can pay him back over time."

Again I was at a loss. "How did you know I'd want to? Didn't you think I'd want to see it first?"

"Of course I did. Why do you think I've been so anxious to see you, to discuss it with you. The chance came up and they needed an answer straight away. You must look at it of course, but I think you'll like it. There's even two bedrooms for when we have a row." He smiled and I kissed the smile. And to think I had been worried that he'd be the one to desert me. Never again would I go to a spiritualist meeting or trust a bloody medium.

We went into a clinch again and would have gone even further had we not been called down to eat. Who needs food at a time like this? But we had to observe the conventions. I'm sure that Katie knew that something was up. Rick, I noticed was flushed and looked excited and I was probably the same.

Such a lot to think about, and to worry about, if the truth be told. I guess I nearly was the unfaithful one and yet it was Rick I always feared would wander first. What does that say about me?

Of course it was Mrs Cook who got it all wrong, but I'll tell you a curious thing. It wasn't Rick but my Mum who let me down. She deserted me to go off with Steve, the man in her life. Did I care? What do you think?

Chapter 4 Playing Away

*Time, they say, is the best storyteller. Certainly it's the only way in which the outcome of events can be truly realized. When Rick and I decided to live together, we had no idea what the outcome would be. We were both eighteen, and in both our cases this was our first real relationship. So when Rick's father offered to put up the money for a flat in Chessingham, money we would have to pay back of course in the long term (and we saw it as very long term) without interest, we jumped at the chance.

"What do you say, Chris?" asked Rick, eyes sparkling in what was evidently gleeful expectation.

"Yes. Yes. Oh, yes," I said.

We had been 'going out' (if I can use that rather old-fashioned phrase) for six months by then, and though there'd been a couple of sticky moments caused actually by mix-ups or confusion over that period, we thought we'd make a go of it. We were influenced probably by our testosterone rather than our brains but, at that age, who the hell cares? I've described him before but I'll do it again, because I love him, I think. Physically quite stocky, a face, much younger looking than his developed figure suggested. Fresh-complexioned with freckles around his nose. His mouth shows the whitest of white teeth. When he smiles immediately his rather ordinary looking face is fantastically attractive in a masculine way. His eyes are green. The turned-up ends of his mouth make comma-shaped dimples just under his cheek bones.

Our flat was on the first floor, small, tiny in fact, and consisted of two bedrooms (one of which was not much bigger than a cupboard – but then we didn't intend to use it) a kitchen, bathroom/bog and a sort of other room, variously referred to as the lounge, the sitting/dining room (by the estate agent), the front room and occasionally the work room. It was also called the sex room because that was often where most of our sex play started – and often finished there too. Though of course we didn't exclude the bedroom, and the bathroom, and in fact the kitchen on occasions.

Jack rabbits weren't in it. We were fucking and licking and frotting and rubbing and kissing and sucking and stroking and humping and blowing and jerking and probing and wanking and coming (oh yes, the coming!) like there was no tomorrow.

Except that there was a tomorrow but when that came we woke up (if we'd happened to be in bed) and immediately went back to doing the same things (or variations of them). After all we were young and full of hormones and testosterone, and the constant opportunities which we had been denied for so long were there and we took full advantage of them. I kid you not.

But I guess you don't want to hear about that.

The flat was in Chessingham, the nearest biggish town to our home village of Elmcombe. Of course I knew Chessingham quite well; I even had my hair done there, but living there was different from visiting. The traffic outside was heavy and though, when we drew the curtains in the evening, we could still hear it rumbling by – so different from the quietness of the countryside. But it was exciting living in what we, perhaps naively thought was a big city.

At the time I was still working as a builder's laborer and Rick was an engineering apprentice, specializing in the design of 'permanent way (trackform and alignment), bridges and tunnels, passenger stations, freight terminals, maintenance and support facilities, and embankments and cuttings' (in other words 'railways'). Rick had learnt the job spec off by heart and I did too and trotted it out proudly if anyone asked what my friend, Rick Harrison did.

My own job was nothing like as impressive and I was determined to get out of the 'tea boy/plaster mixer' rut as soon as possible, but had no idea what I could do. At one time the friend of mine, Kenneth Spiller, a 'real' author who had had his books published, suggested that I might actually be a writer myself and I had started a sort of novel, based on my own life experiences which he had praised. Unfortunately, since meeting up with Rick, my 'authorial career' had been relegated to the back burner because of other more pressing 'burning' desires. Quite coarsely I preferred to roger rather than write, screw rather than scribe. (Rick saw I'd written that last sentence, and told me it wasn't really all that clever – but I'm leaving it in, at least for the present.)

One evening after Rick returned from work. "I've got to go on another course in Southampton for four days," he said.

I worked it out quickly. "That's three nights away," I said. "I won't be able to cope."

Quite rightly, Rick ignored my whining. "It's on mathematics and engineering science," he said, and went on using words I didn't understand and concepts I couldn't recognize.

"Three nights," I said eventually when he stopped.

"You can do some writing. It's ages since you did any."

I was about to whinge on but then I knew he was right. "You'll phone me every evening?" I said.

"Of course." He came and sat by me on the sofa and things fell into place as usual so that I forgot for a while that I'd soon be missing him.

But miss him I did, especially after the evening phone call, but I managed to turn that aching feeling into words and stopped feeling sorry for myself. Once started I found my writing ability returned and there was no stopping me. The words just flowed out, my experiences, my feelings, my 'adventure' with Dominic until I suddenly realized it was past midnight and I felt exhausted. In the morning it would probably read like the worst crud possible but at least I'd been writing again.

Bed was desperately lonely. I stretched out my hand and felt nothing except the cold sheets. I wondered how Rick was feeling, whether he too missed the warmth of another body and then called myself stupid. Of course he did.

Without the usual excuse for staying in bed I was up early in the morning. Over toast, marmalade and tea, I decided that last night's writing hadn't been too bad. In fact I wanted to carry on but of course bossman, Jas, would pick me up in the van and take me off to what I now considered this pointless job with no prospects.

A bit depressed I joined up with the gang and even Alf noticed that I wasn't at my brightest and best. For once though he didn't lay the blame on my losing my boyfriend, for which I was grateful.

Rick rang me early that evening.

"How you doing?"

"Missing you."

"Apart from that?

"Lonely," I said.

"So am I."

"At least you've got company. Well, I assume so."

"A few guys here on the course."

"Fancyable?"

"Not when I compare them with you," he said – all the right things. "If you're lonely, why don't you drop in on the club?"

"And if I meet someone?"

"You'll say, sorry but I'm already spoken for – and leave him with a broken heart."

"I love you," I said.

"Only one more day, after tomorrow."

"And two more nights."

"All the better when I do see you."

And more of this vapid conversation which means so much to two people in a relationship but little to those outside.

* * *

The Olympia Club was Chessingham's only concession to the gay scene - if you discounted the public toilets on the edge of Clarence Park. It had a bar with some stools and a small square place where in the evening couples jumped around, sometimes in time to the music, and finished the evening grinding groins prior to dragging back if they were lucky. The decor was a strange mixture of the original Regency moldings interspersed with some highly colored murals showing scenes of idealized ancient Greek athletes with oversized private parts (very publicly displayed).

We had been several times before and it was a good place for letting your hair down with other like-minded gays. Rick had put the idea into my head and I decided I'd go.

By the time I got to the Club, it was crowded. The small square dancing area was packed with couples, gyrating to a record which, two months before, had been in the charts or at least played on Radio One. Various 'young men' of assorted ages jostled at the bar and tried to catch the attention of Nick, the barman who was on his own and struggling rather. The atmosphere was full of smoke and redolent with a heady combination of sweat and body-splash. In the shadows drugs were on sale, 'disco biscuits' probably, or at least so I assumed when I saw some shifty looking individuals handing over something in exchange for notes.

I looked around for a familiar face.

Then I saw him, a grey haired man still slim and attractive was sitting in one of the chairs around the side of the room. It was my old friend, Ken Spiller, the guy, who if anyone, had persuaded me out of my personal closet, the one that bound me with repressions of shyness and inferiority, and had allowed me to admit to myself that I wasn't a complete moron, that I had a future, even if as yet undetermined, in front of me.

I went up to him. "Ken."

He turned and smiled. "Chris. Didn't expect to find you in a sink of iniquity like this."

"Where's Dominic?"

Ken nodded to an empty seat next to him but didn't answer the question.

"Really good to see you. How's your writing getting on?"

"Fits and starts," I said.

"'Twas ever thus with me. But keep at it. It gets easier after a while."

"Where's Dom?" I repeated. I seemed to be experiencing a sort of reversed déjà vu, if it's possible to have such a thing. My questioning reminded me of when I was quizzing Dominic about the whereabouts of Ken when I was under the mistaken belief that I was getting messages from Ken from beyond the grave.

"Where's Dom?" I asked for the third time feeling a bit like a record that had got its needle stuck in its track.

"He's very fond of you," said Ken.

"And I like him," I said, feeling some sort of response in like vein was expected. And I did like Dominic, had almost fallen in love with him that first time I'd met him as he came charging in from racing across the fields with Ken's dog, Shannon. "Left him in the shop on his own, have you?"

"I wouldn't mind, you know. He always comes back to me and we have a sort of understanding."

I felt completely confused and then suddenly the penny dropped. Ken was offering Dominic for sex, giving me permission as it were.

Dead on cue two people arrived out of the crowd on the dance floor. One was Dominic, dark hair bleached at the tips, expertly done so that it looked natural. Dark eyebrows, the left one raised slightly, quizzically so that I knew he saw everything, life, love, the Stock Market, the glass of Stella, was a universal mischief and could be treated with equal lack of seriousness. He was dragging by the hand a guy with bleached blond hair and eye make-up.

"Ken, this is ..." he started to say and then saw me – and stopped. "Chris! Fancy meeting you."

He dropped the blond guy's hand and kissed me on the lips. I could smell his expensive perfume and feel the heat that came from his body. The blond guy looked daggers at me.

"Ken," said Dominic. "Look after this sweetie for me while I whisk Chris onto the dance floor. You don't mind," he said to the blond who obviously did, "but Chris is an old friend I haven't seen for ages."

I gave Ken a helpless look as I was pulled into the swirling throng, went spinning into the vortex of dancing bodies with the smells of desire and the touches of naked flesh so that my senses whirled. Soon, though, Dominic held me close and I could feel his body, and his excitement pressing into me. He was whispering in my ear. At first I could only feel the soft breath but then I heard the words. "I want you, Chris. I want you naked against me. I want to be inside you." His hands grasped my buttocks and his fingers probed between the crack so that I knew where he wanted to go. He rubbed his groin against mine in time with the music and our pricks made swordplay.

"Dominic," I said or at least attempted to say but it came out in a groan. I tried to say more but his lips had fastened onto mine and his tongue roamed inside my mouth playing cats cradle. One of his hands was on the back of my head holding me there while the other still clasped my buttocks, a finger probing my arsehole. Spitted I was both fore and aft, literally top and bottom.

Did I think of Rick? Hard to say at the time, even harder to think of anything except the passion of the moment. Then I felt a tap on my shoulder and heard a voice say, "I think this is a ladies' excuse me?"

Dominic's blond friend come to reclaim his quarry.

"Haven't finished yet."

But I had.

I detached myself and returned to Ken who had been watching the scene with an expression of wry amusement. He raised his beer glass to me, almost as a salute.

"I already have a friend."

Ken nodded understandingly. "In the first flush of love?"

"Something like that. Tell Dom I'm sorry. And, even if I was free, I certainly wouldn't want to come between you and him."

"Talking of double entendres ..."

I left for home and back to our tiny flat made doubly large by my lack of companion.

In bed I thought about what Ken had said, what Dominic had done and how I had reacted. I'd always admired Ken, considering him wise, the sort of person whose opinion I valued, whose advice I'd take into consideration if not actually obey without question. And yet he had been quite happy for me to have sex with Dominic – as long as Dom went back to him afterwards. Was this the way a relationship worked? Did the same apply to me and Dominic – and Rick?

I knew how I felt about Dominic, or at least how I felt when I was dancing with him, when he was kissing me, when I knew he wanted to fuck me. I knew the lust, the overpowering passion, and I would have done anything for him – or would I? I knew similar feelings with Rick, how, when we were in bed together, when his body was against mine, when his mouth closed on mine, when his cock grappled with mine or was inside me, or mine in him. But, there was a difference. Now I remembered Dominic and knew if I thought about him I'd get an erection and probably want a wank, but felt no uncontrollable longing for him. With Rick ... away from him there was this great wanting, certainly for his body but also for him, for the way he smiled, for the way he touched me tenderly, for just hearing him about the flat, or the lift I felt when I heard his key in the lock and the loss I felt when he shut the door in the morning on his way to work.

This was the difference. Perhaps Ken had been the same once and had lost it or had to bargain with it to keep Dominic with him.

I could smell Rick's smell on the pillow next to mine and on the sheets – and this made it worse – or better, which ever way you look at it.

After a while, I fell asleep.

A Tangled Web

The following morning I pulled a sicky, phoning Jas to tell him how upset my stomach was and how I couldn't guarantee I'd be in control out on a job. He moaned, as he had every right to do, but accepted it.

"Of course you'll lose a day's pay."

"I could expect nothing less, boss. Sorry, I must dash."

I had a plan for the day. Dressed in my smartest suit (in fact my only suit) and a clean shirt and tie, I went into the centre of town and the offices of the local paper, The Chessingham Journal. This was a large brick building with steps up to the double doors, imposing and slightly out of character. I suspected that it had originally been built for a much grander purpose than the offices of a local newspaper.

A young girl, younger even than me and looking as if straight out of school was at the reception desk.

I feared that I might be nervous and start stammering, an affliction I had suffered from for years, but speaking to a child who might have been in the Junior School did wonders for my confidence.

"I'd like to make enquiries about apprenticeships for journalism," without a trace of a stammer.

She gave me a look and I gave her an encouraging smile. Then she started shuffling some papers in a drawer.

"Here's a handout," she said and passed me a printed list headed 'Qualities Necessary for a Journalistic Career'. I looked down the list. Nothing very fearsome there:

- a lively interest in people, places and events
- an ability to write in a style which is easy to understand
- good spelling, grammar and punctuation
- an appreciation of the part a local newspaper plays in the
community
- a willingness to accept irregular hours
- an ability to work under pressure to meet deadlines
- determination and persistence

I think I had most of those.

"Then there's a form to fill in," she said and handed it to me. My heart sank. Under 'Qualifications' needed I saw heading the list the fearsome words: The usual entry requirements for newspaper journalism is a minimum of 5 GCSE passes (grades A-C) or equivalent. However, in recent years it has become rare for a trainee to come into the industry at this level. Over half the recruits are university graduates and many of the others have achieved at least two A Levels or equivalent. One of the passes at A Level or GCSE must be in English. A minimum of two A Levels or equivalent is often required for entry to a full time course.

Shit! Shit! Shit! I hadn't even turned up for my GCSEs at school.

I was though determined not to let the girl see my disappointment.

"I'll bring it back when I've filled it in."

She gave me a patronizing look which probably meant that she didn't even believe I could write but she said nothing. I made as dignified an exit as I could.

I walked back home feeling depressed. I had thought about how I would tell Rick when he came home the following day, how I'd dumped the old 'no prospects' job, got myself something really worth while, something I enjoyed – and now this. Complete failure. Talk about not counting chickens before they're hatched. I had planned on telling Rick with an air of triumph that he wasn't the only one who could better himself and me without benefit of a father's influence.

I tried to convey this in my writing. I had, after all, the rest of the day to fill. Was it worth it? Trying to write? A lonely occupation at the best of times and obviously now without any prospects of financial reward.

Rick was late ringing in the evening. He said that the last full day was always extended and he hadn't been able to get away before.

"I'll be with you tomorrow," he said, perhaps sensing my gloom, though I tried not to show it. "N-O-R-W-I-C-H."

I smiled at the old acronym – Nickers Off Ready When I Come Home.

"Or rather don't bother. I'll rip them off myself."

"Likewise."

"Did you go to the club yesterday?"

"I did pop in."

"Anyone you fancied?"

"Well, Ken Spiller was there, but he's more of a friend."

"And Dominic?'

"Yes," I said, trying to be as vague as possible. "He was there too. He picked up a blond tart and nearly raped her in the middle of the dance floor."

"Not fair on Ken."

I agreed, glad that the telephone hid my own blushes. Never again, I swore to myself would I allow myself to behave in that way, even to put myself in a position where I was alone with Dominic.

I tapped away at the word processor after we had made our tender farewells. Only one more night alone in that bed and tomorrow Rick would be back, would be waiting for me when I got home from work. I tried to put down my thoughts and feelings but they were too personal and I deleted them. Instead I wrote about my ambitions for the future. Even if I couldn't get an apprenticeship as a journalist, and it certainly looked as if that was impossible, I would find something else.

I was just about to decide it was bedtime when the doorbell rang. I looked at the clock on my computer, 11.15 pm, much too late for an ordinary caller. Could it be Rick? Something unexpected happened which meant he could return a day earlier and he'd mislaid his key. The bell rang again impatiently. I'd almost convinced myself that it must be Rick and ran downstairs to the front door, pulling it open to find standing on the front step, not Rick, but Dominic.

He seemed to be very very drunk.

He clung onto the door jamb as if he'd collapse if he let go.

"Chrissy."

I hated being called Chrissy. Always have and Dominic knew it because I told him one time that was what the guys at work used to call me. But what with Dom being pissed and all, I let it go.

"Can I come in?" he said and sort of staggered forward.

Well, I'd just sworn to myself that I'd never allow myself to be alone with him again, but you know, I couldn't allow him to walk into the road and get knocked down by a bus, so I stood aside and he lurched in.

Relieved of the support of the door jamb, he almost toppled over and I had to grab hold of him round the waist. He fell against me and I almost collapsed under the weight but just about managed to hold up. There were two flights each of twelve stairs up to our flat and they looked as difficult to climb as a mountain, but, step be step, we managed it and at last I got him into the room where he crumpled onto the sofa looking up at me with a stupid, almost vacant stare.

I reverted to school mistress mode. "Coffee, I think. Dominic. How did you get yourself into this state?"

I went into the kitchen and started the coffee making. Suddenly I felt two arms wrapped round me and lips nuzzling the back of my neck. Clearly Dominic wasn't as drunk as he had made out.

For the fraction of a moment I felt the old attraction but then I pushed him away. "Leave it, Dominic," I said, and meant it.

But he wasn't so easily diverted. His hands roamed down my body until they reached my groin which he cupped. I felt myself reacting. Not that I wanted to but my cock has a life of its own, especially when it's being fondled by expert fingers, and an erect hardness is being pushed against my buttocks.

I wondered whether I was going to get raped and if it would be a willing, consensual rape but then I felt it was wrong. Here in out flat, Rick's and mine. It wasn't right and I didn't want it.

Again I pushed him away. "No, Dominic," I said and turned round.

He looked at me "You were willing enough last night."

"I didn't have much choice," I said. "Anyway it isn't fair on Ken." Or on Rick, I thought, though didn't say – after all Dominic knew nothing about Rick.

Dominic had a strange, rather strained look on his face. "Ken doesn't mind. We have an arrangement as long as …" He hesitated.

"You go back to him," I finished.

He stood there, swaying slightly, looking uncomfortable, quite unlike the self-confident Dominic I thought I knew.

"Go and sit down, I'll bring the coffee." I felt in charge for a change. He disappeared out of the kitchen.

As I poured the coffee into mugs, I wondered if there was anything wrong. Surely Dominic hadn't come round just for sex. Hay on Wye was over an hour's journey away and there was no certainty that I'd be in if that had been his intention. Dominic, though he might not be as drunk as he pretended, had certainly been drinking – I could smell it on him. And that was unusual for him. He'd drink the odd beer or glass or two of wine over a meal but no binge drinking.

When I took the coffee in, he was sprawled on the sofa. I gave him the mug and sat down in an armchair opposite. He took a sip, grimaced, and put the mug down on the coffee table next to the sofa.

"Sorry, it is pretty shitty. But it'll do you good."

He didn't answer.

"What's the matter? Is there something wrong? Apart from the coffee that is."

His eyes were shut and then I realized he was crying. The tears emerged from under his eyelids and slipped down his cheeks. He made no attempt to stop them with his hands.

"Oh Christ. There is something the matter. What is it?" I'm a sucker for tears. Obviously brings out the mother in me. I wanted to sit by him, put my arms round him, say stupid things like 'It'll be all right. Just tell me what's wrong.'

So I did.

And I held him while he sobbed. Then he put his arms round me and laid his head on my chest. I thought for a moment that this was just an excuse, another play to get me sexed up, but this time was different. There was no overt groping, no kissing, just the crying and the holding as if he needed someone, something to hang on to.

"What is it?" I asked after a while. "Is something wrong with Ken?"

There was a snuffling sound and I hoped he wasn't blowing his nose on my designer shirt, an eighteenth birthday present from Rick. Then I knew that was unfeeling and I decided it could always be washed or dry-cleaned so I clasped him a bit more firmly and stroked his back.

"It's all over," he managed to get out.

I still didn't understand. Then I did. "You mean you and Ken?"

His head nodded furiously and there were more snuffling sounds. I despaired of my shirt. "What happened?"

"We had a row, over Eddie?"

"Eddie?" Did I know someone called Eddie?

"The guy I met last night." I remembered the blond with the makeup who had cut in, luckily for me, when Dom and I were dancing, if you could call it that.

"But I thought you and Ken had an 'arrangement'. It was okay as long as you went back to him."

"But I didn't. I went off with Eddie, and I forgot that Ken and I had come over in my car. I just left him, and he had to stay the night in a hotel. He was well pissed off."

I could imagine. "So when did you have the row?"

"When I got back to Hay this morning. Ken had bussed it back. Of course when I'd finished with Eddie, I remembered I'd left Ken and raced back. We had a blazing row."

"Over Eddie?"

"Not only Eddie. Everyone I'd been with. It seems it had really been hurting Ken, every time I went with someone else. He told me he couldn't put up with it any more – and we'd have to split."

"How did that make you feel?" I asked, falling into the role of a psychoanalyst, or psychiatrist or something (social worker probably).

"I love Ken," he said simply.

"A fine way you have of showing it." That was going too far but I was not best pleased. "All these others. I assume there were others."

He nodded into my chest. "They weren't important, just things to fuck."

I suppose that included me, though I didn't say anything. Eventually I said, "Finish your coffee."

He drank the stuff, then shuddered and said, "It's cold."

"You and Ken'll make it up. How long have you two been together?"

"Six years. Ever since I was nineteen."

"What about your parents? Didn't they freak out?"

"I don't think they ever really realized what it meant, certainly not at first. They were friends with Ken and were pleased that I got on so well with him. It seemed natural to them that he and I should share a house, especially when we became business partners."

"They must be very innocent."

"Or just understanding. Of course they knew."

"He's a lot older than you."

"Twenty years. I guess that's the trouble. I never stopped loving him, just that the call of the flesh was too strong. Younger guys came onto me, and I couldn't resist."

I knew the feeling. I find resistance difficult too. "So what are you going to do?"

He looked at me hopelessly. "I don't know. We've got too much together, the house, the business, apart from everything he means to me. It was only when he told me to get out that it really came home to me."

He'd stopped crying now but he looked terrible. His face was drawn and exhausted.

"What made you decide to come here?"

He shrugged hopelessly. "I thought I could stay overnight, until I could sort things out. If that's all right with you."

"There is a spare room," I said, thinking of the cupboard sized bedroom which neither Rick not I had ever used.

"Can't I sleep with you? I just want to hold someone."

Bad plan! I knew what 'holding' could lead to. "Not a good idea," I said. "You know I live with someone here. We're a couple."

He looked surprised. He obviously didn't know, but then of course, it was Ken I had told, and presumably in their last conversation, that sort of information hadn't come up.

"Where is he?" He looked around as if Rick might be hiding in a cupboard somewhere.

"Southampton," I said. "But he's coming back tomorrow. Probably early."

"It's all right, I'm not going to rape you."

So we carried on talking and I made more coffee, more successfully this time, and Dominic slept in the tiny bedroom while I lolled about alone in the expanse of the double bed.

He left early the next morning. The conversation was limited. He had a hangover and I needed to get ready for work. I hoped that he'd be able to make it up with Ken but I didn't say anything. Time alone would tell.

There were some caustic comments from Alf and Jas as I was pretty tired and could barely stop myself yawning the whole day. I knew I'd have to get another job somehow. Luckily work ended a bit early and I was back in Chessingham by 3.30.

They dropped me on the corner of the High Street. Food was essential. I had to get a meal ready for my returning guy – after what was presumably going to be a boisterous greeting. I called into Marks and Sparks and got some ready meals. They're quite palatable and don't taste like the usual added hydrogenated fat rubbish. A cooling ice cream confection would be good for afters. Trotting back with my arms laden with plastic bags and looking I'm sure like an unusually harassed housewife, I had to pass the Job Centre.

Out of habit I paused to glance at the array of cards advertising jobs in the window – and there I saw it. Tucked into the corner was a job advertisement for the Chessingham Journal. Not anything spectacular, like 'Journalist' or 'Editor' but what was essentially an office boy, no doubt tea maker, filing clerk, perhaps the dizzy heights of photo copying or even 'data entry' – in other words computer typing. I could do that, if I could withstand the no doubt cutting glare of the infant receptionist.

Casting pride to the winds, I went in and, after a wait of about half an hour during which time I worried that Rick might have come home, seen no one was there and gone out again, managed to see a helpful woman who stared at me through thick spectacles but seemed to recognize that I was enthusiastic. She made a call and told me to present myself for an interview the following morning. Oh dear, another day off from Jas and Co., but if I was successful I could say good-bye to mixing plaster for the rest of my life. I had ambitions; I was optimistic.

"Yes, yes," I said. "Thank you very much," and dashed off to prepare myself for my lover.

But I was too late. As I entered the flat someone flung himself at me from out of the living room door. Our bodies moulded into each other with a relaxed, unreserved familiarity. We knew every aspect of each other's bodies but there was still an excitement, enhanced today by the new situation, by Rick's return and my agony of loss.

All at once I felt an almost frenzied elation. I wrenched at Rick's pullover, pulling it over his head. I wanted the touch of skin on skin. I tore at my shirt and the buttons shot across the floor. Rick laughed at my eagerness but then was caught up in the intensity of the passion.

I took the initiative, kicking off my trainers, unzipping my jeans and pulling both them and my underpants off, flinging them aside. Then, deciding that Rick's undressing was too slow, I did the same for my lover, pulling down his trousers, revealing the firm, flat belly, the curly spring of pubic hair into which I buried my face, smelling the clean smell of soap and underneath the subtler, more arousing smell of man.

Rick's erection probed my chin, insistent, demanding attention and I grasped its hardness, gently ran my tongue tip from helmet to spear base before enclosing the head of his long prick in the warm, wet closeness of my mouth. I cupped his ballsack in my hands and delicately fingered the passage between his fork. Rick gave a low moan of pleasure and arched with his hips so that his prick filled my mouth.

I lowered and raised myself so that our pricks were fucked by our mouths. Me in charge. Me dictating the rhythm, speeding the pulse. Then, as the excitement built up, the structure collapsed onto the carpet and we rolled onto our sides, two bodies coiled on the floor, naked as God intended, hands, tongues touching, caressing, stroking to a living flame the two elements of our separate beings, then the coming together in the orgasm.

I came with a great cry and Rick, more quietly, a second or two later.

Afterwards I gazed at the scattered groceries lying around.

"I guess I'd better get us something to eat. You hungry?"

"Only for you," said Rick, kissing me on the mouth.

"We'll do it again later. First let's have some food."

Rick sighed. "And I have to write up a report on the course." We busied ourselves on our separate tasks.

As I stood in the kitchen I looked fondly through the doorway of the living room at the figure of my lover crouched studiously at the table over his work. He was tapping away at the computer keyboard and the words streamed across the monitor screen. For a moment I paused to view the picture, framed as it was through the doorway. I saw the water-color on the wall that Rick and I had chosen together, the light from the table lamp which shone on his silky-soft hair, the way it caught the angle of his cheekbone.

I was reminded of Roberta Flack's song, 'There's more to love than making love.'

Rick was back. There was the interview tomorrow. It could mean the beginning of a new life. I'd tell Rick about it but play it down. After all it's only for an office boy job and I'm not even certain of getting that.

I'm an eternal pessimist; the glass is always half empty. But I tell myself when good things do happen then I'm that much more surprised and pleased.

Chapter 5 Words and Deeds

I wake up the next morning with Rick twined about me, or perhaps it is me who is twined about him. At any rate we are wound around each other amidst a knotted mass/mess of sheets and duvet. There is a leg, and I am pretty sure it's Rick's as I'm not that much of a contortionist, around my shoulder level. My face is sort of buried in some hair which smells pubic rather than any other sort. I haven't had much experience of pubic hair but I do know some is prickly. This is furry, therefore it must be Rick's. And Rick's hand is in the crack of my arse and his body is against me. I rejoice. Rick is home. Rick is home.

Bur this morning I have an interview at the offices of the local paper, the Chessingham Journal, and – my eye catches the digital display on the alarm which we had forgotten to set – it is five to eight, and I haven't even told Jas, boss of the building firm where I work at present (hopefully not for much longer), that I will need another day off as I'm not feeling well.

"Jesus," I shout and jump out of bed – or at least try to but I am all bound up in sheets and Rick and I fall out onto the floor. Looking up I see Rick's startled face peering over the side of the bed down at me.

He grins, reaches out to grab my leg and tries to pull me back. At the same time the front doorbell shrills.

"Ignore it, Chris."

"It must be Jas. You must tell him I'm ill."

"Don't you want to come back to bed?"

"Yes," I say, then, "No, I can't. I've got an interview."

The bell rings again, then continues. He's leaning on it.

"Fuck it," says Rick, and gets out of bed. I'm still trying to disentangle my feet from the sheets. He goes towards the door and I see his naked arse, globes moving enticingly.

"Put some clothes on." But he disappears out of the doorway still naked.

I hear the front door open and the bell stops suddenly. I hear Alf's voice. "Christ, he's got no clothes on." Alf always does state the obvious.

Then Rick, unconcerned. "I'm sorry, Chris is bad. He can't work today."

Jas' voice, cross. "Lazy fucker. That's the second time this week. We can't keep carrying him. Have to let him go. Tell him to get in touch."

I hear the door shut and Rick reappears. This time it's his prick and balls that I see. I'm still lying on the floor but he disentangles me from the bedding, puts me back on the bed and lies on top of me.

"I've got to get ready for the interview," I protest, but not very strongly and it's another half an hour before we start the day properly. Correction, making love with Rick is the proper start to a day but you know what I mean.

So now I'm rushing around trying to look smart. Rick's helping – he doesn't have to get into work until midday – but he's tending to arrange the trousers of my suit and then laughs when the inevitable happens. He does tie my tie – when did I last wear one, I can't remember. In fact I have to borrow one of his, but eventually he gives me an appraising look.

"Scrumptious," he says, which does marvels for my morale but doesn't actually give me confidence as to what a less biased person might think. And there's the awful kindergarten girl receptionist who last time I was there gave me the form which dashed my hopes of becoming an apprentice journalist (not enough qualifications – to be accurate not any qualifications) and she seemed to know it when I said I'd fill it in later.

Now here I am creeping back with an appointment from the Job Centre for what is really an office boy's job. "Look down your nose at her," advises Rick when I express my doubts. "After all what sort of job is a receptionist?"

More than I have, I think, but I'm grateful for his support, grateful for his love and for his kisses on my mouth which I can still feel as I climb the steps up to that ornate portico, so out of place for a small provincial newspaper. I have to force myself to go through the doors, fearing that I'll start stammering and stuttering like I used to do before Ken and Dominic made me realize that I was someone of value, someone who wasn't a total wanker, someone who could achieve a future.

No kindergarten receptionist is going to push me back into that bog of self-disgust, so I step into the hallway and find out that the girl has been replaced by a man. Young guy, with fair hair cut short and a cheeky look on his face. About my age, perhaps a bit older.

"What can I do for you, mate?"

"I've got an appointment with a Mr Fuller. About the office management job." Sounds better than office boy.

"Got a name?"

"Chris. Chris Deacon."

"Got your P45?"

"My old employer hasn't given it to me yet."

"Not told him, I suppose," the guy says with a smile. "I'll ring through to Fuller."

He makes a call and asks me to wait a minute.

"What happened to the girl who was here last time?" I ask just to make conversation.

The guy raises his eyebrows and smiles. "Fancied her did you?"

"Not really."

And he gives me a shrewd look, a look that tells me he probably suspects I'm gay, and I think he is too. So with that as good as settled he says, "Fuller's not a bad guy. His bark is worse than his bite."

"You mean he does both?"

"Sometimes," he says and grins.

His phone rings. He points down a corridor and says, "Second door on the right." Then he says, "Good luck, Chris." I wonder if he fancies me.

Mr Fuller is tall and thin, with dark, untidy hair and big eyebrows that look as if they have got out of hand. His mouth is slightly twisted so that it seems as if he has a permanent sneer, slightly intimidating. I hope I don't start stammering. He is sitting behind a desk with a computer on it. There isn't much else except a telephone, a pad of paper and a biro.

He takes the form from the Job Centre and looks at it, then drops it down on the desk as if it isn't worth much. Probably isn't.

He asks me about school and exams. I wonder whether to bluff it out but decide it isn't worth it. I tell him I haven't got any. He asks why not.

"I was a prat at school. I skived a lot and though my English teacher said I could get a good grade, I didn't even turn up for the exam."

"Can you write?"

"Do you mean am I literate? Yes, of course I am."

"No I meant can you write. Write me a story. Short, 500 words maximum. Now. I'll give you ten minutes."

He provides me with a pad of A4 and a pen and I sit there for a minute wasting time, my mind a total blank. Then I pull myself together, get some words down. A situation, a character, something dramatic which comes out of something ordinary. I scratch out a first paragraph.

How ordinary that day was, how very ordinary the road when Malcolm ran out from the shelter of the buddleia bushes through the park gates, stepped over the kerb preoccupied with his own predicament, disturbed by the circumstances. The car hit him, breaking his thigh, tossing him into the air so that when he fell his right arm fractured.

Then I have an idea. Take it further. Transfer the character point of view to the driver.

Ted, hadn't seen Malcolm, his attention momentarily distracted by a small buzzing insect which had flown into the car. The first Ted knew of the accident was the sound of the impact, the view out of the corner of his eye of flailing limbs and finally the sight of a sprawled body in his rear-view mirror as he sped away.
His heart raced. Why hadn't he stopped, he asked himself. Now it was too late. People would have seen the hit and run, probably phoned for an ambulance, the police, given details. He couldn't return now. He pulled into a pub car park, found himself shaking and went in for a brandy. **Ted** *swallowed it in one gulp demanding a refill.*

And why stop there? Another character, another shift.

Laura, *sitting along the bar observed his agitation. She had her own problem, of course, her depression after being dumped by* **Steve**, *her boyfriend, ex-boyfriend, she reminded herself. She had been sitting in the bar for an hour and drink had now made her bold.*
"You looking for company?" she asked the man drinking brandy and blushed at her temerity. But the man didn't give her a glare of horror, didn't rise and stalk out. Instead he looked at her gratefully. "Let me buy you a drink," he said.

Move on even further. I'm writing at speed now. I glance at the clock on the wall. I still have another four minutes. Move to Laura's boyfriend, Steve.

Steve peered through the door into the almost empty pub. He couldn't understand what had come over him. Only since breaking off his relationship with Laura had he appreciated her worth, her tenderness, and knew his need for her. She'd be in the pub, he thought. He'd apologise. Surely they couldn't be finished so easily by so stupid a mistake on his part.
He saw her straight away, sitting an a bar stool, close to a man, their body postures showing an intimacy, hands entwined. As he watched he saw the man kiss Laura's cheek.
Steve turned and went out. He strode into the park, shaking with anger, staring straight ahead. Finding a seat under the buddleia bushes, he threw himself down, breathing deeply.

And now the clever bit – or at least I think it's clever. Back to Malcolm to give some sort of explanation of that first paragraph.

Malcolm observed the young man come into the park, sensed his agitation but mistook the cause. He misconstrued the gaze Steve directed at him as one of attraction. When Steve sat down beside him on the bench, Malcolm smiled and put his hand on Steve's thigh. Steve started. "You coming on to me?" he shouted. "I'm no faggot. Fuck off."

And finish up as I started. A circular story. Doesn't quite make logical sense but it's satisfying. Well, I think so at least. I scribble the last paragraph, a repeat of the first.

Terrified, Malcolm got up, turned and made for the exit. From behind he heard a shout and quickened his pace. He must get out of the park. He emerged through the buddleia bushes, preoccupied, stepped into the road and was hit by Ted's speeding car. The car hit him, breaking his thigh, tossing him into the air so that when he fell his right arm fractured.

It's finished. I count the words. They seem to be about five hundred. I hand the sheet of paper to Mr Fuller who squints at the writing, but I had to go fast.

He reads, nodding as he gets the point. "And the title?" he asks. "It needs a title."

A few things dash through my mind. 'Merry-go round' or the American equivalent 'Carousel'. That describes the structure of the piece but it doesn't have anything to do with the story itself. "Buddleia Bushes."

"Good."

Wow, talk about writing under pressure.

"And what do you really want to do?"

"I want to be a journalist."

"But you applied for office trainee. Make the tea, do the filing, dig out the stories that someone's hidden somewhere obscure."

"I didn't have the qualifications for an apprenticeship."

Mr Fuller appears to consider, his bushy eyebrows get closer together. He frowns. I've fucked it up, I think. Back to plaster mixing, if Jas will take me back.

Then Fuller's expression clears. "We could do with bright lads like yourself. Pity about the lack of GCSEs but you can obviously write. Bit untrained but there's potential there. Imagination and vocabulary. I'm willing to offer you a position. Any questions?"

So many but I content myself with one. "What do I have to do?"

"I'll start you off by attaching you to a reporter. Follow him around. See what he does, what he writes. See how the office works, how the pieces are filed. You can use a computer I guess. Everyone can these days."

I nod.

"Go and see James Drummond. Tell him I sent you and he's to take you under his wing."

I get up and make for the door. Fuller stops me. "You haven't even asked about money." He mentions a sum which, though not great is adequate, better than what I get for mixing plaster.

"When can I start?"

I think my keenness gives me some brownie points. "Monday." he says. "We'll sort out the paper work by then."

"Could I see Mr Drummond now?" I'm not creeping. I genuinely want to find out what he's like.

Fuller nods. "He's at the Reception. The girl who's usually there had to slip out for a while so he's covering. We tend to cover where necessary."

So that was James Drummond. Well, we'd seemed to get on well when we met. I look forward to telling him I've got the job and that I'm assigned to him. But when I go out I see that the girl is back in Reception. She fetches me a disdainful look. Obviously she thinks I've failed.

I see from that her left tit is called Janice. It has a name badge pinned to it. "I start on Monday, Janice," I say in passing. "Oh by the way, can you tell me where I can find James Drummond? I have a message for him from Mr Fuller."

That's slightly stretching the truth but I feel justified.

"Could be in the coffee bar next door," she says, rather grudgingly I feel. "Jamie's often there."

'Jamie' is it? I wonder if that means they're on intimate terms, or if she just wishes they were. If I'm right about him, I don't think she'll get very far.

"Thank you," I say politely and go.

The coffee bar, Travellers' Rest', (not very original) is indeed next door and I decide I need a cappuccino latte (or indeed a white coffee). If James/Jamie is with a group of friends I'll slip out again, but I see him on his own doing a crossword, so I get my coffee and join him at his table.

"I've been assigned to you," I say, by way of introduction.

He looks up and smiles. "That's nice," he says, and I'm fairly certain he's gay. "James Drummond."

"I know. Mr Fuller told me. Chris Deacon."

"I know. You showed me your Job Centre form."

"Jamie?"

"Not if you value your life. Chrissy?"

"Likewise. I decide we're going to get on. I ask him about himself and the job. He's twenty-four and he's been a reporter for three years. "I'm eighteen," I tell him, "And I've been a builder's mate for one year." And an engineering apprentice's 'mate' for six months, I think but don't say. Then

James says, "I'm just off to an interview. How do you feel about coming along with me?"

"Sure."

James has a car, a rather ramshackle Nissan Micra which has a fair spread of sweet papers, empty crisp packets, wrappers on the floor and seats. There's also a faint smell of dog and some hairs on the back seat.

"Regularly valeted, though I had to sack the last chauffeur a while back."

"Too lazy?"

"Too randy," he says and winks. Well, there we are, an admission. I must watch myself. He's very attractive but I'm very married. I want to mobile Rick and tell him that I've got the job but can't of course while I'm with James.

We drive out to Lockhampton just outside town. On the way James tells me about the story. Apparently the previous night an intruder forced his way into the home of a pair of ladies living together. In spite of his being armed with a knife, the two women managed to overpower him and he was arrested.

"The editor thinks it will make a good story," says James.

"Sounds a bit minor."

"You wait. Spice up the characters, poor helpless pensioners. Insert a bit of drama and it could make front page news. Especially in our little local paper." He pauses then adds, "And when written up by me."

The two women, he tells me are a Mrs Bulstrode and a Miss Pinkerton. I wonder slightly about the relationship between them but don't say anything.

The house, when we arrive, is a tiny 'chocolate box' cottage, thatched roof and all, little windows peering out from under frowning eaves. They've even got a black and white cat sitting on the doorstep which miaows as we walk towards the door.

A large, broad-shouldered woman with slightly more than an incipient mustache opens the door to James' knock. She peers somewhat belligerently at us as if the presence of two young men on the doorstep has somehow sullied its appearance.

"Mrs Bulstrode?"

"Who wants to know?" demands this somewhat formidable creature.

James introduces himself as a reporter from the Chessingham Journal, and includes me in that category.

"We wondered if you wouldn't mind answering a few questions about what happened last night."

The woman turns to look back into the house. "Emily," she calls, "the paparazzi have arrived. Shall we let them in?"

A thin woman with fluffy grey hair and a fussed manner appears. She is made up with slightly inappropriate bright red lipstick and looks a bit worried. She surveys us but presumably thinking we don't look too dangerous, whispers, "You decide, dear."

We are let in and shown into a front room which would have been the equivalent of a Victorian parlor. There are lots of delicate ornaments placed precariously on all available horizontal surfaces. Must have been hell to dust is my immediate reaction.

'Emily' sits on the edge of an upright chair and looks uncomfortable.

James obviously decides that the rather more butch woman must be the driving force so he addresses her.

"Mrs Bulstrode," he says, "just tell me what happened last night."

"I'm not Bulstrode," she says. "I'm Miss Pinkerton. This is my friend, Emily Bulstrode."

Emily giggles. "Others have made the same mistake."

"Apologies. So what happened?"

"We were in bed of course when we heard a noise from downstairs. Thought it might have been the cat but then there were other sounds so we went down. Emily said it might be a burglar"

I imagine them creeping down the staircase, Mrs Bulstrode in the lead – no, that's Miss Pinkerton – again I have them confused (what an inappropriate name for such a Valkyre of a woman) with Mrs Bulstrode fluttering ineffectually behind.

Then the actual encounter with the intruder, he with a knife, the sight of which would no doubt have produced a shriek from Mrs Bulstrode.

"What happened then?"

"He made a jab at me with the weapon," says Miss Pinkerton.

"Using dreadful swearwords," adds Mrs Bulstrode.

"But you managed to get it from him?" suggests James.

"Not in the least, Emily hit him with the cricket bat."

"Cricket bat?" we both echo.

"Yes," says Miss Pinkerton. "She's a brave little thing. She had it with her when we came downstairs, hidden in her dressing gown."

"How did you happen to have a cricket bat to hand?"

Miss Pinkerton answers. "You must have heard of Emily Bulstrode. Played cricket for the Women's Cricket Association England Squad in 1968. That bat hit the final boundary of the game and beat New Zealand."

"I was afraid it might have damaged the bat but it seems the only damage was to the miscreant's head."

James smiles. It is going to be a marvelous story. "Could we take a photograph?" he asks, producing a small digital camera.

"Certainly not," says Miss Pinkerton. "We don't want our faces all over the newspapers."

"I wouldn't mind," says Mrs Bulstrode but Miss Pinkerton is insistent.

"Can I ask your ages?"

"A lady never divulges her age," says Miss Pinkerton loftily. "See them out, Emily. I'll put the kettle on."

As Mrs Bulstrode escorts us to the door, she whispers, "She's seventy one and I'm sixty eight." Then she shuts the door quickly.

"Do you think they're an item?" I venture to ask on the way back into Chessingham.

"That's an area the Journal isn't likely to explore," says James, a little regretfully. "Though it might have added a certain piquancy to the story."

Do I have news for Rick when he comes home? Of course I do and I make the most of it, though back-pedal a bit on James' gayness. Rick is super-pleased and we celebrate in an appropriate manner. Then we go out and have a drink.

Slightly pissed we come home and then I remember I should have rung Jas. I don't really want to but I'm made brave by alcohol. I tell him I'm giving up the job and he's understandably cross. I think he wanted to sack me but I got in first. "You didn't mix good plaster," he says, in a final rather feeble shaft. Then he adds, "Alf will be upset."

I don't understand that. Alf is a dickhead who dislikes me, and the feeling is mutual. Does he mean that Alf won't have anyone to take the piss out of now? Probably. Am I worried? No way.

* * *

The following day is Saturday and even if I still had the job, we wouldn't have worked anyway. Rick and I stay in bed until hunger drives us out and we sit around in the kitchen and eat toast and honey and drink coffee. Later in the morning I go to the newsagent and buy a copy of the Chessingham Journal.

James' report is there though he doesn't have a by-line. He's certainly made the best of the story though and concentrated on how the plucky 'pensioners' (that will upset Miss Pinkerton) got the better of the robber, Mrs Bulstrode laying about with her cricket bat.

"Did she really?"

"So she says. And she's a little wisp of a woman. You wouldn't have thought she'd say boo to a moose. Certainly the guy ended up in hospital."

"He'll probably sue her when he gets out."

"He'll be the laughing stock of his mates if he does."

The phone rings and Rick answers it. "It's for you."

"Who is it?"

He shrugs.

The voice at the other end is hesitant, sounds uncomfortable. I don't recognize it. "Is that you, Chrissy?" Suddenly I do. It's Alf. And he's still calling me the hated 'Chrissy'.

"Chris here," I say, emphasizing the name. "What is it?"

He seems to be put off by my curtness. He's fluffing his words almost as if he's shy. Not like the snide, sneering and scornful person he usually is. "Er ... Jas says you're er ... sacked."

"Has got it wrong, I resigned," I say loftily. "He didn't get the chance to fire me."

"I'm sorry. I'm really sorry. I'll miss you."

Is he taking the micky? "Miss me because there's no one else to take the piss out of?"

There's a brief pause. "I thought ... er ... I thought we were friends. It was just joking. I thought you knew that."

That jolts me back a bit. He sounds genuine. "Course I did," I say, lying through my teeth.

"I wondered ..." Here there's such a long pause that I think he's rung off or dropped dead or something. "I wondered whether we could get together for a drink some time." This last comes out in a rush as if he's gathered up his courage to say it.

I still am not sure whether it's all some sort of joke and that the other lads are on the other end stifling their laughing.

"Well," I say, temporizing.

"And Rick of course."

I'd almost forgotten that Rick had worked with Alf and me and the rest of the gang before he'd got his engineering apprenticeship. "I'll have to ask him."

"I'd like to see more of Rick."

There isn't much more of Rick he could see, after yesterday morning on the doorstep. I wonder whether this is another of Alf's 'jokes'.

"Tomorrow, Sunday? What about the Plough?" he asks.

"Give me your mobile number and I'll let you know."

He does and rings off. "That was Alf," I tell Rick who has been hanging round looking inquisitive. "He wants to have a drink with us."

"He's pulling your pisser."

"I think it may be yours he's after. It was you who showed him everything yesterday morning."

I go to make some more coffee and while I'm in the kitchen, hear the telephone ring again. "It's for you. What a popular boy you are today!"

"Chris, Dominic here. Who was that?" He sounds bright and cheerful, so different from the last time when he had told me that he and his partner, Ken, had split up.

"That was Rick."

"And who is Rick?"

"He's the guy I live with. I told you about him when you slept over."

Again I seem to have stunned my correspondent for there is a pause, then he says, "That's great. Is it the grand passion?"

Unlike with Alf, I can tell when Dominic is making gentle fun. "You bet it is."

"I'd like to meet him," he says. "What about tomorrow for a drink. Ken and I are going away for a week after that so it'll have to be soon. Shall we get together then?" Obviously he and Ken have made it up. I am tremendously pleased.

I have a quick think. If Alf is planning on some sort of practical joke, then us turning up four strong would give us a mean advantage. "Sure," I say. "I'll have to check with Rick of course but what about meeting in the Plough Inn? It's in Cavendish Street, just off the Promenade. About eight?"

"Is it gay?"

"Not until we get there."

I tell Rick that we have engagements for the following day.

"Do I have to come?"

"Yes," I say firmly, and start to persuade him with some strategic fondling. We are getting down to it when the phone rings yet again.

"You answer it," Rick says fatalistically. "It's bound to be for you."

"Hello."

"Chris. It's James, James Drummond, here. Look, I've got to go to London next week to work on a national paper. It's a terrific opportunity though I was looking forward to shepherding you through your first week,"

"What am I going to do?"

"Oh, Fuller will see you're okay. He'll either attach you to someone else or look after you himself."

Well, there's not much I can say to that. I'm disappointed of course but getting in with the editor is probably a good move.

"Tell you what," says James. "Could we meet up for a drink, say tomorrow and I'll answer any questions you might have."

"Sounds good to me," I say, a plan forming in my head. "What about the Plough, eight o'clock?"

"It's a date." He doesn't know how much of a date it is.

"And congratulations on the robbery piece. It reads very well. Good luck with London."

"We've got a party," I tell Rick, and we get back to what I was doing before we were interrupted.

Afterwards I wonder what I've done. But then decide the worst that can happen is an embarrassing confrontation with people who don't get on. And I like most of them. Perhaps we can all gang up on Alf and give him what he justly deserves.

With this mean plan in mind, I give him a ring and tell him the Sunday drink is on.

"Is Rick coming?"

"Sure is."

The Plough isn't much of a pub. There is a bar which runs the length of one wall and on the other side are some tables where customers can eat the indifferent food they serve. If these are full then people prop themselves against the bar or walls or, in extremis, against each other.

There's a dart board at one end and sometimes young men play hazardous games, hazardous that is to other drinkers. At one time the bar used to be full of cigarette smoke but no longer. If anyone wants to smoke they have to go outside and cause a major obstruction on the pavement. It's the Law.

It being Sunday and still comparatively early (a quarter to eight when Rick and I arrive) there are some tables free. We commandeer one, buy some drinks and sit down.

"This is a mistake," I say, suddenly getting cold feet. "Six of us just won't get on."

"Whose fault is that?"

"Mine," I say humbly. "I should never have invited Alf."

"I thought it was Alf who started the whole thing off. He asked you – and me."

"Yes, I find that a bit strange."

"Perhaps he won't turn up. Sort of thing a dickhead like Alf would do. Invite us then just not appear."

"I thought you decided he was going to arrive with the whole gang from work."

Promptly at eight o'clock Dominic and Ken arrive.

In fact this works well. They are obviously anxious to meet Rick, Ken wants to approve and Dominic obviously does. I hope he's not going to make a pass or anything and upset Ken again. I get some more drinks. This is going to be a bibulous evening.

Very soon Ken and Rick are chatting away as if they've known each other for years. Dominic leans forward – he's sitting opposite me – and says, "He's nice."

"He's mine, I'll only allow you to look."

"It's good to have a foursome like this."

"Just you wait. There's more to come."

About ten minutes later James pushes his way through the door and waves cheerily when he sees me. He doesn't seem to be the slightest bit put out by the presence of three other guys.

"James, this is Ken and Dominic. They're a pair. This is Rick. So are he and me." Although he hasn't actually admitted it, I'm sure James is gay and he's obviously quite comfortable with two pairs of lovers. In fact I don't see any signs that he might be disappointed that I have Rick. Am I slightly miffed?

"Well, I don't really feel like a gooseberry."

"There should have been another one, but he's obviously decided not to turn up," I say.

And then, as so often happens at moments like these, when you've denied the existence of something, Alf comes in – alone.

He frowns when he sees a table full of queens. For a moment I think he's going to turn round and walk out but he doesn't.

There is a startled gasp from Dominic and for a moment I see Alf as if for the first time. He's washed his hair and it flops over his (admittedly rather low) forehead. He's wearing a tight black T-shirt (to match his hair?) and his muscles bulge. He looks a bit like I imagine a Cro-Magnon would look like. His legs, in ultra-tight jeans, are slightly bowed. His tackle is very much on show. He looks just that bit embarrassed. Presumably he reckoned on just meeting Rick and me and the increased audience is obviously unexpected.

"And this is Alf," I say, waving him over.

He creates quite an impression. I can see that both James and Dominic are smitten and I even catch Rick giving a quick shufti at Alf's nether regions. Only Ken and I maintain an air of calm detachment.

"Let me get you a drink," says James to Alf.

"Ta." He seems to hesitate and I wonder whether he's considering asking for something really expensive.

"We're drinking beer," I say quickly.

"I'll get the round," says James, and then adds to Alf. "Give us a hand with the glasses."

They go off together. Immediately Dom and Ken demand to know who he is. Rick and I attempt to explain. He's a guy we both used to work with and we always thought of him as a total dipstick, but then he asked us if we'd like to join him for a drink. We left out the bit about Rick appearing naked at the door.

"To be honest," I say, "I thought he was going to bring the rest of the lads along and take the piss out of Rick and me."

"So," continues Rick, "Chris here conceives the brilliant idea that we'll all outnumber them and turn the tables."

"Is he gay?" asks Dominic.

I shrug. "Dressed like that, I'd say yes."

"Certainly James thinks so."

We look across towards the bar where James and Alf are standing next to each other and ordering drinks. As we watch I see James' hand moves to grope Alf's left buttock. There is no reaction, or at least no negative one except that if anything Alf moves slightly nearer.

"I think that answers your question," Ken says.

"But what's he like?" asks Dominic.

"Not the sharpest knife in the cutlery drawer, but he looks dead butch."

"They're the sort that rolls over onto their backs, legs in the air," says Dominic knowledgeably.

Alf's reputation is in shreds when the two return with a tray of drinks. Alf is smiling – so is James. I doubt whether I'll get any information about work from him this time.

It is a convivial evening though Ken and Dominic have to leave relatively early as they have a long drive back. Rick and I also decide that an early night is probably a good idea. After all watching James making eyes at Alf, and Alf obviously enjoying it, isn't that much fun. I guess it's my fault for being such a devious bastard.

Presumably the two of them will go back to James' place and no doubt eventually I'll hear all about it.

So I end the day back in bed with Rick which is where we started. I'm happy with that, and Rick proves that he is too.

* * *

Monday, I get to work on time, in fact I'm early to show I'm keen but I don't think anyone notices. Anyway Mr Fuller comes in at nine o'clock and immediately goes into a private meeting with his staff. Presumably to work out which stories they will follow today. I'm not included, which I can understand but I'm a bit annoyed that I'm told to sit with Janice and learn how to be a receptionist.

More tea making and answering the phone which occasionally she allows me to do, especially when she's doing her nails. Of course I have to ask her what to do with the person who rings up but I guess I'm learning.

People do phone in about their lost dogs – I always thought that was an urban myth. "Tell them to get on to the nearest vet." In a fallow period, Janice asks me about 'Jamie' and how our expedition to the cricket bat pensioners went. I'm quite pleased that I'm able to tell her and also that James has gone to London for the week, a fact which she didn't know and by which she is obviously a bit taken aback.

I think of telling her that he and I had met for a drink on Saturday but I'm not that cruel. Nor do I tell her the probable outcome.

About midmorning, Fuller calls me into his office and I am taken on a tour. There are quite a few reporters, tapping away at their computers, none as pretty as James, not even the glamorous fashion reporter, Nina. Fuller shows me the way a page can be arranged on the screen, text, pictures, headlines etc. and things moved around while the text rearranges itself round the screen. Makes my prehistoric WP at home look so primitive.

When the page is complete it can be sent to the presses at the touch of a key. Brilliant.

I'd like to have a go but he rushes me on and shows me the presses which are in another part of the building.

"You into fashion?" Nina asks, then looks at my poor old suit. "No I can see you're not, but the tie's all right." Of course the tie belongs to Rick. I feel I've failed a test. But she's quite nice and she sends me out to get her an espresso (black, no sugar). I get her a Danish pastry too but she fixes that with a look of complete horror so I eat it myself.

I seem to be with her for the rest of the day. Sometimes she asks my opinion about some aspect of female style but I can see she's not impressed with my babbling response. I do rather like a guy wearing little except a speedo, a skimpy top and sandals and forget myself enough to say, "He's really something."

She gives me a look as if to say, I thought gays were supposed to be fashion conscious, but all in all we get on okay.

Then she lets me type in one of her columns from her notes, but her handwriting is so awful it takes me a while. After that I play with illustrations and headlines rearranging them on the page. Then she points out where I've gone wrong (mostly everywhere) and shows me how she'd do it. I have to agree hers are 100% better but then she's the professional.

At the end of the day I go home and tell Rick I'm fashion editor and he shows me what to do with clothes which is mostly how to remove them, and what to do next, as if I need any instruction in that line of work.

We're lying together in a sort of post-coital cuddle, the sort where we'd be sharing a cigarette if either of us smoke, when the phone rings.

It's the time of day when Rick's mother tends to give him a ring. Mine doesn't of course because she doesn't know where I live and I'm not broken hearted over that.

Rick picks up he receiver and immediately says, "Hello, mum." He leans across me so that he's lying on my chest with his buttocks in the air. I idly stroke them. "Oh," he says, with a sudden change of tone.

Oh dear, I think, something's wrong. I carry on stroking sympathetically.

Then he says, "Long standing relationship? How can you say that after so short a time?"

His mother has broken with his father, I decide. She's found someone else - or perhaps it's him who's found someone else.

"Condoms," says Rick. "Of course you'll need condoms."

What the hell! Changing tactics I express my disapproval with a sharp slap. A rosy blush appears.

"Ouch!" Rick turns to face me. "It's Alf." Then he speaks again. "Yes, of course you can. Any time you feel you need to talk." He puts the phone down.

"Alf? I thought it was your mother."

"Obviously," he says, rubbing his bottom.

"What did he want?"

"Advice. He thinks he's in love with James. He sees a long term future with him."

"After a single one night stand? I always said he wasn't the brightest squib in the firework display. What was that about condoms?"

"He asked whether he needed them if it was going to be a long term relationship."

I can scarcely believe it. "Alf? Dipstick Alf?"

"It's rather sweet really. I wonder what James said to him."

"And I won't be able to find out until next week."

By the end of the week, as well as being a reporter's assistant, a backup receptionist, a fashion guru, a digital compositor, a filing clerk and a tea boy, I begin to feel at home in the offices of the Chessingham Journal. I'm enjoying myself. Okay I've made an enemy for life of the tit named Janice (who thinks I'm about on the level of some nasty many-legged insect) and one of the older reporters who decides I am getting preferential treatment from Mr Fuller but if I can put up with bullying bosses like Jas and imbeciles like Alf, I can put up with anyone.

Except that Rick has decided that Alf is a sort of fairy tale youngest son who has just been on a quest and discovered a Prince with whom he will live happily ever after. I point out that things like that rarely happen outside the pages of Hans Christian Andersen or the Brothers Grimm, and even then there are unpleasant endings for some of the characters, especially those with flaws in their personalities – which both Rick and I know Alf has.

I am looking forward to James' return. For one thing I want to be out with him interviewing people and possibly having a hand in writing up stories for the paper.

For another, both Rick and I are getting heartily sick of Alf's constant ringing up, asking whether we've heard from James (we haven't), seeking our advice as to how to approach James when he does come back. (Flat on your back with your legs in the air and your knickers off, I suggest, but only to Rick) and forestalling his attempts to come round (and presumably talk about James). My God he really has got it bad.

Saturday comes. One of the disadvantages of the new job is that the newspaper doesn't sleep at the weekend so some staff have to be in on Saturday and Sunday. We get the choice of either, plus a day off during the week in lieu. Means of course that I can't be with Rick for the whole of the weekend but we make up for it on the days that we are together.

So that Saturday I'm on and when I get into Reception suddenly someone leaps onto my back, puts his (I assume it's a him) hands over my eyes and says, "Guess who?"

Having just about suffered a heart attack, I'm not too pleased but I turn round and it's James.

"You bastard. I might have died from shock."

"Good front page cover story. Cub reporter dies in newspaper attack."

"Tell me all about London."

"Come next door for coffee."

"Is that okay?" I ask, not wanting to take liberties so early in my job.

"Thought you'd been assigned to me," he says. "You're my slave. You do anything I want." He gives me a look which I find difficult to interpret. Is he joking?

Janice (the tit) comes in. "Tell Mr Fuller I've taken Chris with me," says James. "On assignment."

"Right you are, Jamie," she says, and I see James flinch. She's not doing her cause any good by calling him that.

Over coffee (James' shout) he tells me about London, how impressed he is with the National Dailies (he was with the Daily News – a redtop tabloid, and spicy), how that's where he really wants to be, he's decided.

"What about you? How did the week go?"

My account is not as exciting but I save the best until last. "Talking about slaves. You've got a fan who's just about nuts over you."

James' eyebrows shoot up. He looks so much like a caricature of astonishment that I almost laugh. Then he smiles. "Oh you mean Janice. I'm sorry I'm afraid she doesn't stand a chance."

"Not Janice. Alf."

For a moment his face registers incomprehension. "Alf?"

"The guy you had last Sunday or at least I assume you did. The one we left you with at the pub. The Plough, remember. Short, dark and well-endowed."

His expression clears. "Oh Alf." He laughs. "Nice enough kid, but I didn't 'have' him, as you put it. I invited him back but he refused."

"He's been ringing us every day since, saying how much he's in love with you and how he wants it to be a permanent relationship. I tell you he's absolutely serious, lovesick."

"Oh my God."

"I'll tell you, you'll have to sort it out or he'll drive us mad."

James looks doubtful. "I'll do what I can," is the best I can get out of him. "I have a bit of trouble with shy cock-teasers."

Then we get down to work. James has several assignments. The local football team (league somewhere near the bottom) is rumored to be sacking its manager. Find out what is happening. Complaints of near riot condition at the poor end of Chessingham. Are the yobs holding the tower blocks to ransom? A more or less local author has just published a book which is creating waves. Is it the next Man-Booker prize winner for fiction?

"Your decision," says James. "Which one do we do first?"

I consider while James finishes his coffee. I wonder whether I'm being tested. "My liking of football is limited and my knowledge of it is practically zilch. So my instinct is to put that last. On the other hand it might be best to get it over and done with first."

"Fair enough."

"Then the investigation into the seamier side of Chessingham sounds as if it could be a bit dangerous, so do that next. Finally the interview with an author sounds like the tranquil end of a day's work."

"Except of course that all three will then have to be written up." He raises an eyebrow.

"Of course," I say blandly.

The football goes quite well. We interview the manager who says the chairman has complete confidence in his ability and there's no truth whatsoever in the rumor. One of the ground staff who wishes to remain anonymous, says the manager is a 'complete wanker' and won't last out the next two weeks, especially if the team lose both times. As they're playing two of the best teams in the division, that sounds most likely. We manage to get hold of a player who says that confidence in the manager is at rock bottom and to his certain knowledge the chairman, whatever he says, is looking around for someone else.

"It's really quite fun, isn't it?" I say afterwards as we climb again into James' Micra and make our way towards the dodgy end of town. Here, two tower blocks, Wentworth and Bailey', stand like sentinels to an internal open space covered with litter, dog shit and the rusting detritus of a consumer age, supermarket trolleys, a burnt out car, a 'dead' fridge and some very stained mattresses. It is not a pretty sight.

Some kids looking slightly sinister in hoodies stand around. I'd prefer to give them a wide berth but James goes right up to them. "Hello, guys," he says and they look at him with something like amazement, as if they're not used to anyone speaking to them except perhaps to tell them to 'fuck off'.

"I'm a reporter from the Chessingham Journal," James says. "What's it like living here?"

The kids look at him, then look at each other. One with torn jeans and muddy trainers says, "Crap." He can't be much older than seven or eight. His voice is high and fluting.

"In what way, crap?"

"There's fuck all to do," says one.

"They just tell you to fuck off," says another.

"Who's they?" asks James sympathetically.

In answer the kids turn and point at the flats, rows and rows of terraces with doors and windows in identical and apparently endless repetition.

"Aren't they where your parents live?"

Grudgingly they nod, though one mutters, "Ain't got no fucking parents."

"Don't you get bored, doing nothing all day?"

That does strike a spark. There is much energetic nodding of hoods.

"What about school?"

"School's crap," says our original informant.

"Will we be in the paper, mister?" asks another.

"Do you want to be?"

"As long as you don't put in our names."

"Okay," agrees James.

"What about him?" asks one pointing at me. "Don't 'e talk?"

"He's a listener," says James.

"'E's got big enuff ears," says the observant little bastard.

"We're going to talk to some of the people in the flats."

"Don't talk to mine," says jeans and dirty trainers.

"Nor mine," say the rest.

"Okay," says James. "Which ones are yours?"

They're not so savvy as they think as immediately they give the numbers of the flats where they live, "Fifteen." "One hundred and thirty seven." "Ninety three." The litany goes on. It's a sad list.

Obediently James writes down the numbers in his book. "Can you look after my car? See that no one touches it. I'll pay you."

"'Ow much?" asks an incipient entrepreneur.

"A fiver," says James, then adds, "When we come back."

But they're not that stupid. "Nah," says one. "We've been caught that way before."

"Two quid now and three when we come back and the car's OK."

The deal is done, the money passed over.

"Whew," says James. "I wouldn't like to live here."

We enter a tower block. The lift looks as if it's out of action. Certainly the door is buckled, so we climb some steps. We try number thirty seven because we can hear a child crying inside and assume someone is there to look after it.

After a while there is a shuffling sound and the door opens a crack. A girl's face appears. She is probably no more than thirteen.

"Is your mum in?" asks James.

"Oo wants to know? Are you the p'lice?"

"No, we're reporters from the Journal. We'd like to speak to your mum."

"She's in bed."

"Is she ill?" We can see an emergency rescue in the offing. Good story.

"Nah. She's asleep."

But she isn't because a voice comes from somewhere inside. "Oo is it, Letitia?"

Letitia shouts, "Sez they're reporters."

"What do they want? 'Ave you let them in?"

James can see this going on for ever, so he shouts, "We're doing an article on the state of the Tower blocks. We just want to ask you what your opinions are."

"They're crap," says the voice. Then, "Hang on, I'll be down."

We wait while Letitia observes us through the crack in the door. Then eventually she is replaced by an older version which looks at us suspiciously. James waves his ID card and at last the door is opened wide enough for entry. It's surprisingly neat inside.

"I'm sorry to disturb you. Your daughter says you were in bed. I hope you're not ill."

"Of course I'm not bleedin' ill. I work nights, that's all. Sleep during the day, but it's time to get up now. Come in. What do you want to know? Letitia, make some tea."

We are led into a small living room. There is a sofa, a bit scuffed but comfortable enough and a huge plasma screen TV set. Some magazines of the 'Hello', 'OK' sort lie around on a glass-topped coffee table. The carpet doesn't look old.

"Sit down, then," says the woman.

We ask her name but she's reluctant to give it even after we promise it won't appear in the paper. Of course we can probably always find it from the electoral register – if she's actually on it.

"So, what's it like living here?"

"Nothing for the kids to do. They run around in gangs and after dark it's dangerous to go out."

"You have to," I point out, "if you work nights."

"I can look after myself, but I don't allow the kids out. Then there're fights between rival gangs and races round the ring road with stolen cars. You must have heard of the big fight last Saturday."

"Yes, indeed," says James. "That's what prompted our interest. Can't the police do anything?"

"Police. They're worse than fucking useless."

Letitia comes in with some mugs of tea on a tray and a plate of jammy dodgers. The tea is very weak and very sweet.

"Who are the gang leaders?"

Letitia's mother suddenly became reluctant to talk, but after a bit of persuasion admitted that one was called Stan. "He's a right little bastard. Draw a knife on you as soon as look at you."

"Nasty," says James. "And the other one?"

"Not quite so bad, but a dangerous lad. Named Alf."

That bring us up short. Of course it's coincidence. Must be. "What's he look like?" I ask.

"Dark hair. He's nineteen. He's actually got a job, builder's laborer I think. Shame. Needs taking in hand."

"Do you know his surname?"

"No, and if I did I wouldn't tell you." I think she's lying.

"Do you think he'd talk to us?" asks James.

"Doubt it. He lives in the other block, Bailey. You can ask there. Everyone knows him."

We finish our tea, wondering how it will affect the state of our teeth, say thanks and leave.

The boys have formed a ring round the car, guarding it apparently because it doesn't seem to be damaged in any way. James gives them the remaining three quid.

"Do you know Alf?" he asks casually.

"Alf Leyton?" says one boy and suddenly they all freeze. Obviously he has let out something he wishes he hadn't.

James wants to go to Bailey Tower but I suggest that's not a good idea. "That's Alf's name," I say. "We don't need any more confirmation, and anyway I don't think these guys will want to look after the car now you've paid them."

On the journey back to the centre of town, we discuss this development. "Is it really the same Alf?" James asks.

"His name is Alf Leyton. I knew he lived somewhere in that part of Chessingham because Jas always complained about having to take him home and the fact that he feared for the safety of his van. It must be the same guy."

"In a way that makes him even more attractive. He's dangerous as well as sexy."

I sigh, giving up the argument. "He's yours to sort out. Just get him off our backs and do what you want with him. My advice, have nothing more to do with him – once you've dropped him."

James changes the subject. "There is one more problem," he says. "This author we're supposed to interview. He's one of those shy, retiring ones. Doesn't give interviews, hates all reporters. Lives a quiet life, reclusive almost to the point of being a hermit somewhere near Wales – at least as far as publicity is concerned."

"So how do we get in touch?"

James shrugs. "I guess we just have to try. The only thing I have is his telephone number. Ring him on the mobile will you. If I get caught while I'm driving, I could lose my license."

He passes across a slip of paper. I look at the number and it seems strangely familiar. "What's his name?" I ask.

"Kenneth Spilling."

I laugh and James turns to stare at me in astonishment. "What's the matter?"

"I know him," I say. "In fact of course you've met him. Same day as you met Alf. Ken, of Ken and Dominic, is Kenneth Spilling."

"You never told me his surname. You never even mentioned he was a writer."

"Never came up," I say. "I'm sure he'll talk to me though. We've been friends for some time. It was he who started me on my decision to become a journalist, to write anyway. Only thing is, I know so much about his private life that I don't know how much I can tell for publication. If he wants to be private, then what can I tell you?"

"I know he's gay. But that's not the sort of thing the Journal publishes. Just ask him if he'll chat to me about his new book. We've met socially after all."

I laugh. "Except that you were feeling up a teenage gang leader at the time. Okay, I'll give him a ring."

I can tell that Ken isn't all that enthusiastic. I have to try a bit of blackmail on him. "Because of you, I'm starting a career in journalism," I say. "And now you won't help me with writing an article on a future Booker prize winner with your latest book."

"What did you think of it?" he asks.

"I haven't read it yet." James though is nodding. "But James has."

"James?"

"You remember James. From the Plough. The one who was after Alf."

"Ah, that James. Is he with you now?"

"We are in his car. He is my – " I don't quite know what to call him. "– my mentor. I'm the trainee."

"Does Rick know?" His tone is playful.

"Of course."

"Okay. I'll talk to James. Get him to phone me when it's convenient." I raise my thumb to James as I ring off.

It's been a long day and I'm feeling exhausted after helping James write up our articles. Actually there's still some work to do on the Alf and Ken stories but James tells me to go home.

At the flat I collapse on the sofa while Rick busies himself in the kitchen. "I need some TLC," I complain and he comes in with some drinks. He sits down and I rest my head in his lap. I tell him what we've done today and of how Alf and Ken figure in the stories.

"That's an incredible coincidence," he says. "If not two incredible coincidences."

"That Ken's book has been nominated or that Alf lives in an urban slum?"

"That you should get those two stories."

"Just luck," I say, and move my head so that it rubs against his groin. "Forget all that. This is where I want to be."

I turn my face so that I can kiss a rising erection. At that moment the front doorbell rings.

Rick makes as if to get up, but I say, "Leave it. We're not expecting anyone." The bell rings again.

"They'll know we're in," says Rick. "The light's on and the curtains aren't pulled."

I groan but let him up. He goes out into the tiny hall and I hear the front door open.

"Oh," says Rick, in a mixture of surprise and perhaps regret.

"Who is it?"

"Alf!"

Alf is about the last person I want to see but my recently born reporter's feeling come to the fore. Okay we can check on the story, perhaps find out some more.

"Bring him in."

He slouches in. He isn't wearing his 'I'm gay and I don't care who knows it' skin-tight jeans but a looser pair. His T-shirt is covered by a hoodie, the hood thrown back – perhaps his 'I'm the leader of the gang' outfit. His black hair is rumpled and untidy. He has a dark mark – a bruise? – over his left eye. He looks rakish and slightly sinister.

Our cans of lager are on the table. It seems uncouth not to offer him one. "Nothing stronger?" he asks. His voice is a bit slurred and I wonder whether he has been drinking already.

"There's a bottle of whisky in the cupboard," says Rick. His father had given us one when we moved into the flat. Not being whisky drinkers, we hadn't actually opened it.

"That'll do," says Alf ungraciously.

Rick gets the bottle, opens it and pours him a glass and he drinks it then holds out the glass for more. I wonder whether it's wise to.

"Nice to see you," I say, though it isn't. "Did you come round for anything special?" He doesn't answer, just sits and looks into his glass.

Rick puts a CD on to cover the silence. It is Justin Timberlake, not my favorite but marginally better than James Blunt. We sit for a while, then Alf reaches out and refills his glass. I waggle my eyebrows at Rick and he says something to the effect that he has to look at our meal cooking in the kitchen, He takes out the whisky bottle with him. Alf doesn't appear to notice.

"Well, Alf," I say putting on my reporter's hat. "I didn't realize you lived in Bailey Tower. What's it like there?"

This rouses him a bit. "Crap," he says, reminding me of the young kids we were with this afternoon. "Unless you're the boss."

"James and I were down there today."

"James?" Has he forgotten him already? Then he smiles. "Oh James. He's sexy."

I agree.

"I like him," he says and takes another swallow from his glass. He suddenly staggers to his feet and starts swaying in time, more or less, to the music. "Dance with me," he says.

I go to him and he clasps me close so that I can feel his body. He breathes whisky fumes into my face. We sway together for a while and I can feel him getting hard. "What do you mean, you're the boss?" I ask.

He laughs, pushing his groin into mine, then backs away. "Fuck, it's hot," he says and pulls off his jacket and drops it behind him like a stripper. He's dancing, swaying to the music and doing it well. Before I realize it, he struggles out of his T-shirt. His body is good, well-defined. His hand goes to his groin, finds the zip of his jeans and pulls it down. His jeans slip to his knees and he fiddles with the gusset of his briefs.

"Hang on," I say.

"No, you hang on," he says and offers his cock which is nicely erect and sticks out of his flies.

Rick chooses this moment to come back into the room. I shrug helplessly as if it's nothing to do with me, which it isn't really.

"Leave you a moment with anyone," says Rick, "and you have them stark bollock naked before you can say Hatshepsut."

"Hatshepsut?"

"Some old queen, Egyptian I think."

Alf, noticing that he is no longer the centre of attraction, says, "What about a threesome?"

"Tell us about being the boss," I say.

This is the wrong thing. "You do what I say. Suck my cock." He waves it suggestively.

"What are we going to do with him?" I ask Rick.

"I've phoned James. He's coming over."

"Meanwhile ..."

Then the alcohol or possibly it's just inertia takes over, for Alf suddenly crumples onto the sofa, assumes a foetal position and drops off to sleep. Rick fetches a blanket and covers him.

Ten minutes later James arrives.

"What's the panic?" he asks.

We indicate the prostrate lump on the sofa still covered with the blanket. James looks under it. "Did you have to strip him first?" he asks.

"Self inflicted," says Rick. "I think he was grieving for you."

"And that involves removing his clothes?"

"Takes different people in different ways. Well, he's all yours now."

"I can't take advantage of him in that state."

Alf's eyes open. They see and focus on James. Alf holds out his hand. "Jamie," he says and I see James flinch but it doesn't stop him from being pulled to join Alf on the sofa. There is fumbling of clothes and I suggest to Rick that this is not the place for us.

"I'll see he's all right, safely delivered home, either his or mine," says James. "See you tomorrow."

In our own bed Rick says, "So that's what his cock looks like."

"Not as nice as yours," I say, and kiss it to prove it.

"Nor yours," says Rick replying in kind.

Tomorrow I will carry on with my new job writing words about other people's deeds but tonight I lie with my lover and the world can go hang.

Epilogue: Alf's War by Kenneth Spiller

Kenneth Spiller was in the throes of composition, always for him a painful business. He ran his fingers through his greying but still thick hair so that it stood up in tufts. His fingers tapped on the computer keys and then with a stifled curse he selected the paragraph he had been agonizing over, and with two key strokes deleted it.

Dominic, his partner, both business and life, looked up from the book he was reading. "Problems?" he asked sympathetically.

Kenneth had once been a prolific author turning out novel after novel each year, but then had given writing up for some years. Later he'd returned and written a hugely successful novel which had been short-listed for the Man-Booker Prize. Now he was writing a sequel – or at least trying to for the process was slow and obviously painful.

"I can't get into the main character," he said. "He won't come alive. Too many facets to his personality, I think. He seems to be three different people in one."

"A bit like Alf Leyton."

Ken's frown disappeared. "Yes, that's it. A gang leader in a rough estate, a gay guy and someone with an ordinary everyday job. That's it exactly."

He started again on the paragraph which was giving him so much trouble. All seemed to go well and then he stopped again. "I'd like to find out more about the real 'Alf'."

"Fancy a bit of rough, do you?"

Ken smiled. "I've led a very sheltered life."

"So what brought this on?"

"I want a lad who's gone wrong but has a softness inside. I sensed that in Alf the time we met. I need him as a character in the book."

"But we only saw him for a while, and then he was making sheep's eyes at that reporter fellow, James Drummond. All I saw was a hardness in his jeans."

Ken nodded. "There's much more to him than that."

"You ought to go and see him. Tell him you want to put him in a book. He'd jump at the chance. He thinks he's God's gift, you know."

"Do you think so? As I said, I think he's more than that. Anyway I can't traipse down to a housing estate and start interviewing people. I'd probably get beaten up."

"Arrange to meet him in a pub, like we did last time. Chris will probably be able to organize it for you."

"It's an idea. Perhaps I will."

* * *

A crowd of enthusiastic kids stood around the burning car with the rapt attention as if it were a fireworks display. It was well alight now and flames were shooting out of the windows. Someone shouted, "Get back. It's going to blow." The watchers withdrew to what they assumed was a safe distance and there was a sudden pause, everyone waiting, until with a whoosh, the petrol tank exploded accompanied by a cheer from the audience.

At the same time a siren sounded and a fire engine arrived, much too late to do anything to save the car. All they could do was douse the flames. Then a police car turned up to more derisive cheers. As two officers got out, the kids melted away into the darkness, disappearing into the surrounding flats of the tall tower blocks.

One young man dressed in jeans, T-shirt and the ubiquitous hoodie, stood on a third floor balcony landing looking down on the scene. His hood masked most of his face but suddenly throwing it back, he revealed a pale face, thick eyebrows, thin lips twisted into either a smile or a sneer, it was difficult to tell which. His hair was cut short. Only his grey eyes looked less than hard.

After a few minutes watching the flames die down under the stream of water from the hose and the two policemen chatting to the fire officer who was obviously in charge, the youth descended the stairs and walked across the open space between the two tower blocks where the car's skeleton still smoked and steamed. The reek of petrol and burnt plastic hung in the air.

One of the police officers hurried across to him, yellow jacket lit by the street lamps. "Oy you," he greeted him. "Can't you see there's been a fire. It could still be dangerous. Keep back."

"Course I seen it. I watched it from up there." He waved in the general direction from which he had come. "It's them bloody kids from Wentworth Tower." He turned and pointed to the block of flats on the other side of the space where the car stood. "They want putting away. Ain't safe for us round here anymore."

The policeman looked at him warily, suspiciously. "What's your name?"

"Alf. Alf Leyton. 325, Bailey." The answer was candid, seemed to be innocent, the eyes open, but the policeman had learned not to trust anyone from the estates.

"How d'you know that it was the lads from the other block?"

"Seen 'em, didn't I? They drove in, set it alight and then ran into Wentworth."

"You didn't do anything?"

"What could I do? Piss on it from the landing?"

"Any names?"

"Couldn't make 'em out clear like, too dark and they was all wearing hoodies. But it was them."

The other policeman called his partner over.

"I've got your name and address. I'll want to speak to you again."

"Be my guest," said Alf. Skirting the burnt out car, he went towards the main road. As he reached it, he was joined by another youth dressed in similar fashion. They fell into step together.

Alf's plebeian job was one which he hid from his mates at home. They knew he had a job of course; it was impossible to hide that but they didn't know what he did. Most of the others drew their weekly unemployment benefit and spent it on drink or smack. Some of them had been awarded Anti-Social Behavior Orders which they 'wore' with pride.

Alf's second in command was called Biff. He was shorter than Alf. Like him he wore his hair cut short and it didn't really suit him. His eyes, a washed out blue, and his lips in a permanent sneer. Most of the time his drug habit kept him functioning. If he was unable to get a fix he became unreliable which was a simple way of describing the sweating, shaking, sick creature that he turned into. Alf disapproved but he and Biff had grown up together since primary school and, though neither of them had attended much secondary education, they had kept together and now, through loyalty, they were, at least in terms of the gang, inseparable.

Biff's need for smack and Alf's passion for sex meant that they were times when they went their separate ways. Neither enquired into the whereabouts or doings of the other though Alf probably knew more about Biff's dealings than the other way around.

"What did the pigs want?" asked Biff, who seemed in a mellow, rational mood.

"The obvious."

"And you told them?"

"I told 'em."

"Enough so they'll get onto Stan?"

"Hope so, though the police aren't all that bright. But I've got a contact with the local paper. The reporter will find out what the police don't."

The newcomer laughed. "Brilliant. Coming for a drink?"

"Not tonight, Biff. Gotta date."

The other seemed disappointed but accepted the excuse. "See ya, boss."

Alf made his way through the buzz and bustle of the streets towards the centre of town. After the excitement of the arson attack, Chessingham settled down to its normal evening activities. There were people around and it seemed that Alf didn't want to be recognized. He kept the hood up and when he passed anyone coming the other way, he turned his already half hidden face away. But he met no one he recognized or at least no one who recognized him.

He moved into the area or what had once a couple of centuries before been the fashionable area of the spa town. Here elegant Regency houses formed a quadrangle inside of which were grass-covered squares with perhaps a cedar tree in the middle or bordered by a verge of graceful silver birches. Of course the houses were no longer owned by a single owner or if they were, they had been split up into flats so that perhaps six or seven separate individuals or families occupied the three floors.

Alf arrived at the doorway of one such house. By the side, just under the triangular portico seven names were listed beside bell pushes and a speaker system which could be operated from the individual flats to open the front door. Alf pressed one which was printed neatly with the name J. Drummond. As if his arrival had been expected a voice immediately answered sounding distorted through the speaker.

"It's me," said Alf, gnomically.

"Come in, 'me'." A buzzing sound accompanied the opening of the door. Alf pushed through into a hall painted light green. There were separate doors to right and left and a staircase which led upwards to the higher floors.

James Drummond's flat was at the top of six flights of stairs. The door was open and as Alf went in, James enfolded him in his arms and kissed him.

It had originally been the attic servants' quarters of the house in Cadogan Square, and, perhaps unusually, had been converted in a sensitive and attractive way. The ceilings sloped to follow the incline of the roof and the dormer windows looked out onto the grassy square invisible of course at this time of night though giving a pleasant view in daytime. A bedroom, a living room, kitchen, bathroom, small but tastefully furnished.

There wasn't much reticence, at least on Alf's part. He was flushed with the success of his plan and this translated itself into sexual excitement. He grabbed hold of James' shirt, pulling it over his head. He needed the silky feel of naked skin on skin. "Slow down, tiger," said James laughing at the other's eagerness but then himself was caught up in the frenzy of lust.

Alf took the initiative, kicking off his trainers, unzipping his jeans and pulling both them and his underpants off in one movement, flinging them aside. Then, deciding that James' undressing was too slow, he did the same for his lover, pulling down his trousers, revealing the firm, flat belly, the curly spring of pubic hair into which he buried his face, smelling the clean smell of healthy sweat as well as the arousing smell of man.

Like a young animal, which of course was exactly what he was, Alf rooted in the undergrowth for his prey, found it and fastened upon it, licking and sucking, then, raising James' legs he buried himself further in the moist darkness, lubricating with his tongue the passage where he wanted to be. James understood and was willing, opening himself to probing tongue and then fingers which expanded the entrance.

Only when Alf seemed to want to enter unprotected, did James demur, insisting that he must wear a condom, putting it on himself when Alf seemed to be in too much of a hurry to unroll the thing. Once on, Alf plunged in and James, sensing his need, restrained the cry of pain and protest that the sudden entry had so nearly forced out of him.

Alf came quickly and James stopped him when he tried to wank him off afterwards in response. "You needed that. It was obvious. I'm all right."

They lay together on the bed but Alf was not in the mood for post-coital cuddling. He shifted nervously then sat up and said, "I want a drink."

"We'll have to go out," said James. "I haven't got anything in."

Alf seemed about to insist then sighed. "Doesn't matter."

"What was it tonight? You've never been like that before."

Alf turned his head to look at him. "Did I hurt you? I'm sorry." His almost skinhead haircut made him look hard but his eyes were soft. Suddenly he looked much younger than his nineteen years and James was moved to tenderness.

He said, "There's something wrong, isn't there?"

"Nah. Everything's good." He laid his head in James' lap and looked up at him.

"What is it then? Alf, Chris and I were down at your place the other day. It's almost gang warfare isn't it?"

For a moment Alf looked guarded. "You been spying on me?"

"I'm a newspaper reporter. It was a story."

Surprisingly Alf laughed. "There's another one tonight. Car set alight. You want to ask around Wentworth Tower block but mind yourself. They're a tough bunch. Don't go down there alone – and don't go down at night."

"Wentworth? That's Stan Rackley's territory, isn't it?"

"Not for long if I have anything to do with it," said Alf.

James' reporter's nose twitched. "Tell me more."

* * *

The sky was a startling blue and clear. Everything looked washed clean after the night's rain. Even the square of grass between the two huge concrete blocks, grey and impersonal, appeared fresh. Only the blackened skeleton of the car which hadn't as yet been removed had a curiously surrealistic look to it.

"There you are, Chris," said James. "Just as Alf told me."

At the base of the Wentworth Tower block a police car was parked and as the two reporters watched, they could see a couple of policemen moving along the landings, knocking on the doors and occasionally getting answers. Unlike the previous occasion there were no kids hanging around. Presumably the presence of the police had scared them off or at least made them wary that they might be questioned about not being in school.

"Shall we talk to the police?" asked Chris.

"I think we'll try Letitia Stone's mum. She tends to keep an eye on things and we've already established a sort of rapport."

"She'll be in bed. You know she works nights."

"Maybe."

They walked up to the third landing of Bailey's Tower and knocked on the door of number thirty-seven. But it was Letitia's mum who opened the door. This time she was dressed in jeans and a T-shirt and looked amiable if not over pleased to see us.

"Oh God. It's you again. What d'you want?" Though she said it with a bit of a smile.

James waved at the remains of the car. "Any ideas as to what happened down there, Mrs Stone?"

"What do you think? Spontaneous combustion?" Obviously she had had some good education. Chris wondered how it was that she'd ended up in this place of horror. Her husband's desertion? Children to support? A job which brought in little more than peanuts? What had she said last time? Working as a club hostess? That didn't sound too bad, but the term might have hidden a multitude of meanings.

"You'd better come in." She wasn't bad-looking, thought Chris. A trifle harassed but with delicate features and unruly golden hair. If I were straight, I might even fancy her. She couldn't be much older than her late twenties.

"Give us a break," said James. "What happened here last night?"

"What you see is what you get. What do you think? Load of kids set light to a car."

"Nothing happens here without either Alf's or Stan's say so."

"Oh you know that do you?"

"We know who's in charge of the gangs," said Chris.

"He speaks!" She turned her attention to Chris. "Okay. I guess one of them gave the orders – and tried to blame it on the other."

James' contribution. "So if the police are going door to door in Wentworth, Stan Rackley's territory, that would mean it was Alf Leyton's idea."

"You're a mite too sharp. Could be dangerous for you spreading ideas like that."

"I know Alf. He wouldn't actually hurt anyone." Then James thought of the force that Alf had used the previous night and wondered if that was true.

"Tell us more about Stan," said Chris.

"That's one mean guy you don't want to mess with."

"Okay. That's a given. What else?"

Mrs Stone hesitated. She was obviously reluctant to say too much. Did Stan's influence extend to this this tower block, or perhaps it was because Letitia was a vulnerable young girl. Then, suddenly, it burst out. "He's cruel. He enjoys causing pain to others, and they won't complain because they're all shit scared of him."

"You don't mean Alf?" James remembered Alf's strange mood the previous night. Obviously something had happened to him. Could he have been the victim of one of Stan's sadistic actions? Yet there was nothing on Alf's body as evidence, no bruises, no cuts. He dismissed the thought.

"No, Alf's got his own protection. Stan Rackley, I'm afraid, tends to pick on weaker kids, or the old and helpless. The pensioners round here are frightened of him. I think he takes most of their money each week. And I've seen young kids beaten black and blue who won't say a thing about how they got injured."

"That's outrageous!" suddenly James realized he was sounding like an apoplectic colonel rather than a rational journalist. "Something should be done about him," he said in a more reasoned tone.

"Don't you think we've tried? And more often than not regretted it afterwards."

"The police?"

The expression on Mrs Stone's face said it all. Clearly she considered the police were either in league with Rackley or as scared of him as the others in the area. They could obviously descend on him mob-handed but if they didn't have any evidence, and no witnesses were prepared to come forward, they weren't going to be successful.

"What about Rackley's family?"

"He lives with his mother. Poor woman!"

"Stan mistreats her?" James sensed a story.

"Not really. It's just that she has to put up with the hatred of the people in the blocks. I feel sorry for her. I don't think she's got a single friend."

"There's not much point in trying to talk to Stan?"

"I wouldn't advise it. Any questions will probably just lead to violence, and you'll come off the worse."

Outside Chris said, "Well we didn't get too much out of that."

"We'll just have to concentrate on Alf. And I can do that."

* * *

"The police and your reporters aren't doing fucking much," said Biff later that evening.

"Patience," said Alf.

Friday night and the Hastings Arms was full. Biff was agitated. He couldn't seem to sit still. His face under his cropped hair was flushed and his hands clenched and unclenched around the neck of his beer bottle.

"We ought to do something about Rackley."

Alf touched one of Biff's hands as if to steady it. "We will, Biff. We will."

"When?"

"Soon." He spoke soothingly but it didn't seem to calm Biff. His fingers drummed on the table top. "I'll go and see what my reporter friend has to say. There'll probably be something in the paper tomorrow."

Biff looked up. "I'll come with you."

Alf shook his head. "No, I'll go alone."

Biff looked as if he was about to protest but then he shrugged. "Suit yourself." He looked around as if to find someone else he knew. It wasn't difficult. The pub, the Hastings Arms, was if anything a stronghold of Bailey Tower gang members. No one from Wentworth, if he was under twenty-five, would dare to come in and certainly not on his own.

"Don't do anything stupid."

"Sure you want to go by yourself?" His expression was almost pleading.

"He'll talk to me if I see him alone." It was true though of course this wasn't the reason he wanted to see James by himself.

Biff watched him leave the pub, saw him exchanging remarks with various people on the way.

Alf hadn't been gone much more than ten minutes when the door swung open and Stan Rackley himself came into the pub. There was an audible gasp from the drinkers but Rackley wasn't alone. He had a pair of 'bodyguards'. thick, brutish lads with fighters' noses, one on each side of him, and some more guys, not as thickset but looking as if they'd be useful in a scrap.

Rackley himself was tall, and, though not thin, looked as if he didn't have a spare ounce of fat on his body. He was dark, obviously of mixed blood, and spectacularly handsome. He could have been a model on the catwalks of any famous fashion house. He wore jeans and a vest which exposed his arms and his chest which was muscular and tightly defined.

He looked around the pub now silent as if seeking someone, but failing to find the one he wanted he fastened on Biff, walking towards him with light steps, the feet of a dancer, firmly balanced yet able to spring in any direction if need be.

Biff flushed even more deeply and stood up, his thighs bumping the table so that his beer bottle toppled and the contents spread over the surface. Short as he was, he had to look up to stare into Stan's eyes.

No one spoke for a moment, then Biff said, his voice higher than usual, "What you doing here, Rackley? You ain't welcome in this pub."

Rackley spoke, his voice low and controlled and on the face of it polite. "I was looking for Alf but I see he's not here. Perhaps you could give him a message."

Biff didn't answer.

"Did you hear me, Biff, a message for your boss."

Biff nodded sulkily.

"Tell him, I don't like him trying to set the pigs and the gutter scribblers on to me. Tell him that, will you ... poodle." The last word a scathing insult.

He turned and went out followed by his entourage.

Biff, in contrast to earlier had gone white. For a moment he didn't seem to know what to do, his hands grabbing hold of the top of the bottle. Then he made up his mind, spoke to a couple of his friends and all three of them went out into the darkness.

* * *

That Saturday morning Chris didn't have to go to work on the Journal so he and Rick stayed in bed doing what they both did when getting up early wasn't essential (and sometimes indeed when it was) making love.

They played like puppies together. Rick rubbed his body and tickled him around the waist so that Chris was forced to squirm and respond. He could feel his lover's cock, hard and thrusting, against his stomach and knew that his was erect as well. Rick could not keep still. Like a young animal he worried and played with Chris uttering little whimpers of enjoyment. First his head was under Chris's arms and he felt a tongue licking the bushy hair, then in an instant Rick's head lay on his stomach and his teeth were gently nibbling at his skin. Meanwhile one hand was on his chest, the fingers playing with his right nipple while the other hand crawled up the inside of his thigh until it reached just below his scrotum. Chris was entranced; it was as if he were in bed with at least three people. He tried to respond by grabbing hold of him but Rick would not allow himself to be caught, first rolling aside and then almost immediately rolling back to mould to his body all the way down, lips kissing his, chest and stomach joined, Chris's legs under Rick's, Chris's cock imprisoned - happy captive - in the moist fork between the boy's legs.

Now Rick was quiet and still, his lips gently grazing and then the point of his tongue emerged, insistently probing inside Chris's, past his teeth, into the mouth and meeting the other tongue, tasting the saliva, joining the two tongues. It was as if this inspired a fresh urgency in the groin, each pushing against the other, Rick's hands cupping Chris's buttocks, the middle finger of his right hand now exploring the deepness of the cleft until it found and entered the crinkled hole. Chris gasped. He was aware of what Rick wanted and knew that this was what he wanted too. Rick was taking the initiative. Chris felt another finger inserted and both moving, enlarging the hole. He opened his legs and then raised his knees so that the access could be easier and the fingers probed deeper. Now Rick's cock had found the cleft and Chris raised himself up even further, Rick's body between his legs, his cock piercing the sphincter, sliding in, lubricated by its own clear juice.

Again there were little animal noises gradually rising to a crescendo of excited yelps and Chris pushed against him and felt the boy's tense body straining, the passion building up and then the orgasm pulse and pulse inside him. Rick shuddered and collapsed onto him murmuring his name again and again.

So it was late when they got up and had a necessary shower. In fact Chris was still in there when he heard Rick's shout from the kitchen where he was making a late breakfast. "There's been trouble on that estate you been going to. Someone's got hurt. Stabbed."

Chris wrapped a towel round himself and came out. The news was still on the radio, a reporter outlined what was known about a fight the previous night which had resulted in one teenager being stabbed and who was now in intensive care in the local hospital. Several others had had wounds, either from a knife or broken bottles, but their injuries weren't, it was thought, life threatening.

"Who's the one that was badly hurt?" asked Chris.

"Someone called Bernard Duffy, apparently."

"Never heard of him. I wonder if James has. I'll give him a ring."

Chris heard the tone which went on and on until he decided that James must be out. Then, just as he was about to ring off, the phone was answered.

"James, have you heard the news? There's been gang warfare down at the tower blocks. Someone in intensive care."

"Who is it? I've got Alf here. He'll know him if you've got a name."

"Guy called Duffy, Bernard Duffy."

Chris could hear James passing the name on and then, in the distance, Alf's shout.

"Christ, it's Biff. I told him not to do anything stupid. Where is he?"

"Chessingham General," said Chris.

"I'll be in touch," said James and rang off.

* * *

Alf hated the smell, the look of hospitals. Outsides were bad enough, rows of windows behind which people were sick and probably dying. Inside, all antiseptic and white paint. Staff moving around purposely on errands of dire horror or carrying vessels which probably contained body parts or worse.

The receptionist, though, who saw Alf and James was plump and sympathetic. She looked Bernard Duffy up on a computer screen. "You won't be able to see him," she said. "He's under constant supervision and you're not relatives. The last report on him was that he's stable."

"We're friends," explained James.

The woman nodded sympathetically. "You can go and see the ward sister," she said, "though I doubt she'll be able to tell you much more at the moment. De Montfort ward." She pointed to a sign which showed the way. "Just follow the signs."

They ran along corridors. It seemed a long, long way but eventually they came to a pair of swing doors and a sign over them which read, 'De Montfort Ward'. In a little room to the right there was a card which could be slipped in and out. It read: Sister Yvonne Grant.

They knocked and a woman, brisk, efficient-looking asked them what they wanted.

"We're friends of Bernard Duffy," said James.

"His parents are with him at the moment," she said. She pointed across the ward where there was another room and a window in the wall. They peered through the window. Biff lay in the bed, his eyes closed, his head enveloped in a bandage. His face under the white cloth looked much younger than his twenty-two years. His eyes were closed and around the right one spread an ugly red bruise. There was a dressing on his neck and another over the top part of his chest. Tubes came from his nose and arm and a drip stand stood beside him. A green blip on a VDU screen traced out the spidery green evidence of Biff's life. As each one progressed across there was a 'ping' audible even to them outside. It was almost all that showed he was still alive as his breathing was so shallow that his chest barely rose and fell.

"I'll get that bastard, Rackley," muttered Alf.

Outside he rushed off in the direction of the towers and though James called after him, he didn't stop.

* * *

After the fight the previous night, the police were down at the blocks in force. The word had gone around and all knives and anything that might constitute a weapon had disappeared from the flats so the house to house produced only kitchen cutlery and DIY tools which either had nothing to do with the incident or had been impeccably cleaned.

An atmosphere of brooding suspicion and hatred was almost tangible. A few guys stood on corners and glared at anyone from the opposing tower or sulkily replied to police questions with comments that ranged from the 'Don't know anything about it' to 'Try the other tower block, guv'.

Alf's arrival caused a sudden stir. A few people, youngsters mostly appeared from their front doors. Some curtains, in those windows that had them, twitched. Alf didn't seem upset.

A policeman saw him from one of the lower balconies and gave a shout. The copper's face had a jaundiced look, not exactly yellow, but with a pissed-off expression which suggested that he didn't think much of the world in general and his job in particular. Too much paperwork and bureaucracy no doubt.

"Mr Alfred Leyton," he said on reaching ground level. There was more than a hint of sarcasm in his tone.

"The very same."

"I assume you know something of the fracas that happened here last night."

"I heard about it on the radio this morning."

"Do you mind telling me what you were doing last night."

Alf appeared to consider. "Well, I was in the Hastings Arms early on, then I left about ten as I had to see a bloke about a dog."

"You left at 10.10," said the policeman. "You were seen on CCTV."

"You mean there's a CCTV camera watching the pub?" His eyebrows raised in mock amazement.

The policeman refused to be drawn. "About ten minutes later Rackley and his mob arrived and there was a bit of a 'conversation' with a friend of yours, a Bernard Duffy. Rackley went out, again observed on the CCTV and a bit later so did Duffy with some of his mates."

Alf nodded.

"Unfortunately the camera only observes the car park and the fight started on the road outside. Can you give any information on what happened next?"

"No, mate," said Alf. "I was off to meet a friend of mine, reporter on the Chessingham Journal. We had some drinks and I crashed out there.

He'll confirm it. Another friend phoned us to say that Biff, Bernard Duffy, had been injured and we went to the hospital to see him. They'll confirm that too."

The policeman looked a bit baffled. "Was there any bad blood between Rackley and Duffy?" he asked.

"Looks like it, dunnit."

"Anything specific?"

"Ask Rackley – but don't believe anything the bastard says."

"We have. His mother says he was in all evening after the visit to the pub."

"Your marvelous CCTV show him going home then?"

The policeman shook his head.

"So much for fucking technology."

* * *

But it was via new technology that Alf got in touch with Stan Rackley. Neither of them had regular mobile phones with accounts, too easy to trace, too easy for the police to find out when and where calls were being made. Generally they managed to 'find' one when necessary, either mugging a kid on his way back from school, using it for the purpose and then scrapping the SIM card.

But Stan's mother had one and Alf, through devious means, got hold of the number. So it was that in the afternoon while the sun shone outside and an opposite darkness reigned within in the minds and hearts of the majority of the Towers' inhabitants, Stan's mother handed her son the phone.

"It's for you."

"Rackley," said the voice which Stan immediately recognized, "I understand you were looking for me last night. Well, I'm here now."

"You want some of what we gave Biff?"

"I don't use a knife," said Alf.

"Chicken!" Stan's tone was scathing.

"No. But we can do a chicken run."

"To prove exactly what?"

"Who's the best!"

"And the winner?'

"Takes all. Boss of both the estates."

Rackley laughed. "And the loser just gives in."

"The loser," said Alf, "will lose the respect of his gang. He'll have to give in."

There was silence as Rackley obviously considered this. "Where's the race?"

"The circuit. The ring road round Chessingham."

"Okay."

"In opposite directions!" said Alf.

* * *

Why had he added that last stipulation, Alf wondered. It would be easier to race round in the same direction knowing where the opponent was at all times, seeing him draw ahead or drop behind and being able to compensate. Then he knew that that was exactly the reason. It would be too easy. Going in opposite directions would mean there'd be no way of knowing where the other was, except of course that they'd pass half way round, not until the last possible moment when they arrived back at the starting point and they'd know for certain who had arrived first, and who had lost.

His mind went back to his relationship with Rackley. They had never been friends. In fact one of his earliest memories was scrapping with him in the junior school they had both attended and having to be pulled apart by a teacher. And the severe bollocking they'd got from the headmistress afterwards. He remember she had forced them to shake hands and how their eyes had blazed furiously while their lips had mouthed the hated words, 'I'm sorry'.

Later Rackley in his teens had formed his own gang made up from the youths of his tower block estate and to rival it Bailey block had retaliated with their own gang, at first under the leadership of Biff. But Biff had been weak, too often incapable of making decisions and thus it was that his best friend, Alf had taken over. Shrewd, occasionally quixotic, taciturn, loyal to his mates, and dogged in his pursuit of what he thought to be right he was the ideal boss.

Words had to be got around to the Bailey boys of the Chicken Race. Ordinarily Biff would have done that but now it had to be Alf himself. A car had to be 'obtained', stolen from somewhere in town, obviously as powerful a one as possible and everything in place by two o'clock am – when traffic was at its lightest on the ring road around Chessingham.

He would not tell James. James had failed him in his plan to find out enough for the police to take action against Rackley. Now it would have to be Alf on his own. And he would beat Rackley. He knew it. All he needed was a car, one that preferably wouldn't be missed until the following morning.

The car had been parked at the side of the road at a meter which still had most of an hour to run. Alf had spotted immediately that the driver had left his keys in the ignition. He could scarcely believe it. What a tosser he must be. A car like that, dark blue, sleek as a bullet, black leather seats which, Alf knew, would clasp like the embrace of a lover. It didn't need much thinking about, just a quick look up and down the road - there was no one in sight who could possibly be the owner of such a car - open the door, get in and away.

He eased himself into the driver's seat of the Lotus Elan, twisted the ignition and smiled as the engine purred into life. He let his right foot press gently on the accelerator and felt the power surge even though the tone of the engine barely rose. He put the gear lever into first and released the clutch. The car moved sweetly away from the curb. He changed up and saw how the speedometer almost immediately touched forty! What a feel. This wasn't a car. It was indeed a lover. It held him like James did from behind with legs and arms wrapped round him. And sexy too. The slight reverberations from the engine gave him an almost instant erection.

All he had to do was to hide it until tonight, and that was easy. There were garages under the tower block, some of which were empty. It wouldn't take much to break open a padlock, get one of his boys to keep watch, and it would be safe until needed.

* * *

Tension was high on the estates. The word had got around as was intended and the members of both gangs (or at least all those who could escape their parents at that time of night) were out in force.

It was raining by midnight, a light drizzle which, though almost invisible, soaked anyone outside. The only way it could be seen easily was in the headlights of cars or underneath the street lamps where it shone as an almost transparent curtain.

Alf's mobile rang. It was James who was worried that he hadn't seen or heard from Alf since he had run off from the hospital that morning. James had expected Alf to come round in the evening. When he hadn't turned up by midnight he had become seriously alarmed. The news on the radio and TV couldn't have been worse. At ten o'clock it was reported that Bernard Duffy had been moved back to intensive care. At eleven o'clock the report came through that Biff had collapsed and died. And then finally James rang him. Alf's voice sounded strange and rather strained.

"Are you all right?" asked James. "I was expecting you."

"Things to do."

"Please, Alf, don't do anything stupid." It was the same request that Alf had made Biff before leaving him alone to be stabbed by that arsehole, Rackley.

This though prompted Alf to ask. "Have you heard anything about Biff? How he is."

So Alf hadn't heard. James wondered what to do. Should he tell him? Certainly he'd find out soon enough but he thought it would have been better to tell him face to face. Then at least there would have been an opportunity for comfort. The pause though had alerted Alf to the fact that there was something wrong. "Have you heard anything?" he repeated.

"I'm sorry. Biff died this evening. It was on the news."

There was a long pause.

"Come over, Alf. You need company."

Then came the dial tone, the sound of a disconnected line.

* * *

A Tangled Web

The gangs came out in force to watch the start. Alf drove up in his Lotus Elan to the applause of the Bailey Boys. The car engine purred quietly as they waited. Alf stared out through the windscreen while the wipers swept from side to side. He didn't speak to anyone.

A couple of minutes later Rackley arrived in a Porsche 968. There would be two very irate car owners that evening and presumably the police alert for two missing high performance, very expensive cars.

They waited on opposite sides of the road, facing in opposite directions. Rackley leant across from his driving seat and shouted something through the window, probably a taunt but Alf ignored him. The drizzle was illuminated in the beams of their four headlights and had formed black viscous looking puddles in the road. Hit one of those at speed and the car would slide out of control, aqua-planing.

No one had decided how to start the race but all of a sudden Rackley revved up his engine and shot off. Startled, Alf did the same and saw the red rear lights of his opponent grow fainter in his mirror and then disappear as the road bore round to the right.

At the moment there were no other vehicles on the road but as Alf pushed his accelerator down to the floor, he quickly caught up a car going slowly in front of him. Alf swung the car to the right and overtook. The driver realizing that Alf was breaking the speed limit sounded his horn but Alf paid no attention.

Biff was dead. Biff was dead. The refrain sounded in his head, and Rackley or one of Rackley's gang had killed him. He mustn't be allowed to get away with it. Beating Rackley in the race would, he was sure bring to an end the reign of terror.

The leather seat clasped him firmly and Alf was once more reminded of James. But he mustn't think of him. He had to concentrate on the road. The street lights flashing past his head exerted an almost hypnotic influence and the dark patches in between seemed almost like a temporary blindness.

This was a dual carriageway with occasional islands and roundabouts. Here Alf had to stand on the brake and swing the car round, tires screeching. He couldn't allow his speed to drop below an average of 60 or 70 mph. On a straight passage he coaxed the speedometer to just over

100 mph. In this car it didn't seem very fast until he tried to round a bend and found he was struggling to control the car. He found himself sliding towards the embankment on the left and only just managed to avoid crashing into it.

Even so he did not slow down, overtaking the occasional other vehicles on the road and ignoring the flashing of their headlights and the sound of the horns. He knew the road but at this speed the familiar landmarks came along unexpectedly and Alf swore as he slithered into yet another skid this time almost completely crossing the road.

For a moment, when he pulled back onto his own side of the road, he couldn't understand where he was then he recognized the large building ahead of him and realized he had travelled almost a quarter of the way round the circuit. He wondered where Rackley was. He wished he had said more to James.

But Biff was dead. Biff was dead. It beat a refrain in his head which mapped the swishing of the tires. Only braking slightly to take another roundabout, skidding round it while at the same time overtaking another car doing the same maneuver, interrupted the flow.

Accelerator, brake, accelerator flat on the floor. Biff is dead. He could have saved him if he hadn't gone to James, spent the night with James, left Biff on his own to battle it out with Rackley and his gang. He was responsible. He shouldn't have left him. Biff had asked him not to.

A car coming the other way flashed its head lights. For a moment Alf thought it might be Rackley but it was going much too slowly and the flash was only a polite request for him to dip his own. Ignoring that, Alf sped past, throwing up a spray of water as he passed. Soon be half way. Then he'd know how he was doing. Foot down. Road bridge marked nearly half way. It flashed by and for a moment the rain ceased then continued as he came out the other side. Where was Rackley?

Then the twin beams of a car coming the other way lit up the sky, blinded Alf as the came towards him. Had he passed half way? It was difficult to tell. And suddenly Alf didn't care about the race, about who could win, about the gangs back on the estate.

With frightening speed the two cars closed.

Alf gritted his teeth and swung his car onto the other side of the road.

"This is for you, Biff," he said and drove straight between the headlights.

* * *

Dominic looked up from reading the type on the screen. "So that's what happened," he said. It was almost a question.

"That's what might have happened," said Ken. "This is fiction you know."

"And we can find out?"

"Ring up your friend, Chris. Get him to ask how James and Alf are getting along together."

THE END

Table of Content